Aoife Carr.

WHAT ABOUT IT, SHARON?

What's gone wrong with Sharon? To look at her you'd
think she was just an average teenager – height medium,
hair medium long and medium brown. But there's no
happy medium for Sharon at the moment. Everyone is
trying to push her in different directions and none of the
ways is where she wants to go. And it's hard to be left out
and ignored, or teased and taunted where it hurts most –
like the time when her alleged 'friends' find out about her
non-existent date.

It's no better at home, where she simply can't talk to her
parents. So when things reach crisis point, the new bright
£5 notes in her mother's purse seem to offer Sharon one
solution to her problem – and when that fails a bottle of
aspirins suggests an even more dangerous one.

Ironically, it is only after tragedy has struck a girl who
has shown kindness to her, that Sharon starts to face her
problems realistically.

This is an honest and sometimes overwhelming story of
a confused girl who knows there's more to life than she's
being offered – if only she can find it.

GW01003186

Aoife Carr
                  124 Seafield Rd
                        Clontarf
                        D-3

Tel: 338062
age: 14
Date: 11/2/86 .

What About It, Sharon?

John Harvey

Puffin Books

Puffin Books, Penguin Books Ltd, Harmondsworth, Middlesex, England
Viking Penguin Inc., 40 West 23rd Street, New York, New York 10010, U.S.A.
Penguin Books Australia Ltd, Ringwood, Victoria, Australia
Penguin Books Canada Ltd, 2801 John Street, Markham, Ontario, Canada L3R 1B4
Penguin Books (N.Z.) Ltd, 182–190 Wairau Road, Auckland 10, New Zealand

First published in Peacock Books 1979
Reprinted in Puffin Books 1982 (twice), 1984

Copyright © John Harvey, 1979
All rights reserved

Made and printed in Great Britain by
Hazell Watson & Viney Limited,
Member of the BPCC Group,
Aylesbury, Bucks
Set in Intertype Baskerville

Most of all, for Kay and Liz

I

Debbie Bradley was a bitch. A right little bitch! Walking round town with him like that. Strutting across from the fountain to the bus station on those stupid high heels of hers. It's a pity she didn't fall flat on her face, like the time she did when they went up to London on that visit. Down Oxford Street, she'd gone, flaunting herself like Lady Muck and wham! She'd gone sideways on one of her heels and fallen right over in front of everybody. Her coat had got ripped, she'd grazed her knees through her tights, and when she'd been helped up, she'd almost burst into tears.

Serve her right, silly cow!

If Mick had been there . . . if she'd done it today when she was with him, then he'd have looked at her differently. Instead of which . . .

Sharon sat up and pushed her hair away from her face. Parted at the centre, medium length, medium brown, it was forever falling across her eyes, ends catching at the corners of her mouth. It's the way you sit, Sharon, her mother said, always hanging your head like that. Look up, girl, look up for a change.

Sharon looked up. The walls and roofs of Stevenage dipped away towards the town centre; on the right the squares and rows of her own estate were laced through with the tops of trees. She was sitting near the edge of the park, close to the pavilion and the swings. A man wearing a bright red sweater was walking diagonally across the football pitch, holding a dog's lead in one hand. Ahead of him, a tatty brown and white mongrel was running in tight circles, stopping every now and then to brace his forelegs and bark shrilly.

She continued to watch as first the dog, and then the man,

disappeared from sight beneath the tunnel that would take them under the road to the houses on the far side.

Sharon fingered her hair again, twisting a length of it round and round. What had she done wrong? What had she said? What hadn't she done, more like.

'Come on, Sharon,' he'd said, 'don't be a pain.'

Then, after another five minutes of trying, he'd stood away from her and stared, annoyed and uncomprehending: ''Smatter, Sharon? What you got to be so tight about?'

She remembered the sudden cold feeling that had run through her seeing him like that, hearing the words repeating and repeating. She'd regretted it then, wanted to, wanted him to get hold of her again. Well, why not? Everyone else did. All of her mates. To hear them talk, it was the easiest thing in the world, just part of going out with a bloke.

But she hadn't been able to say anything, not then, not with Mick standing there looking really pissed off: she'd known it was over.

Over! One night at the pictures, a couple of evenings in a pub on the other side of town in case her dad saw her and got mad, and a Friday at the Mecca.

Over – it hadn't started.

'C'mon, Sharon, I'll walk you to the bus station.'

Great! All the way across the road. He'd leant up against the shelter as though pretending he wasn't with her at all. As soon as the double-decker had pulled in he'd mumbled something and walked off.

Nothing like making it obvious.

Serve her right for hoping he'd give her another chance; ask her out again. She'd been thinking about that earlier that morning, in the town centre doing her shopping. She'd been standing in line in Littlewoods, waiting to pay for the bacon and cheese her mum had told her to get, and suddenly Debbie had come rushing over to her, along with Heather and Janice and Carol.

All tarted up and shrieking at the tops of their voices.

Making a right scene they were. Everyone turning round to look at them. They loved it, of course.

''Ave a good time last night, Sharon?'

'Yea, we saw you down the Mecca with 'im.'

'Bit of all right, isn't 'e, Sharon?'

They squealed with laughter and Sharon went red and wished they'd go away and leave her alone.

'Come along, young lady,' said a middle-aged man behind her pompously, 'you're holding up the queue.'

Sharon moved forward, hoping that he hadn't noticed Carol and Janice making faces at him.

'That your dad, Sharon?' said Heather loudly.

'You know it isn't.' Sharon felt herself getting even hotter, redder.

She'd shuffled along, banged her basket into the back of the woman in front, who'd turned round sharply and stared at her as though she were a bit of dirt. The other girls had giggled; laughed into the backs of their hands: Carol taller and thinner than the rest, at least four inches taller than Sharon, who was supposed to be what was called average height. Debbie was the shortest, less than five foot without her heels, her heavily made up face pretty and sharp.

Before Sharon had got to the check-out, Debbie had come up to the rail and said in a half-whisper: 'You goin' to see him again, Sharon?'

'I suppose so.'

'Don't you know, then?' Mockingly.

'Yea. Yes. Tonight. We're going to Letchworth. To the pictures.'

She stood her ground under Debbie's stare, aware that she was blushing furiously.

'See you then, Sharon.'

'See you.' 'See you,' they'd chorused and pushed their way through the other Saturday morning shoppers, laughing and talking, heads close together.

'Nice friends you've got,' said the woman in front.

Sharon had said nothing, just clutched the plastic-coated wire handles and willed the queue to move faster. She was angry with herself for letting them get on at her like that. What did they matter? Enough for her to lie to them.

Not that it was the lie that worried her : what did was that she'd be found out.

What Sharon hadn't realized was how soon; she hadn't known that Debbie and the others had already heard Mick's side of things. Not until she'd left the shop and seen them by the fountain.

The fountain was in the middle of the pedestrian precinct, set in a square below the bus station. On a Saturday it seemed the busiest part of the town, shopppers hurrying past, youths sitting on the low wall calling out to their mates.

They'd been there along with Mick and another boy called Terry. As soon as she'd come in sight, Debbie had begun pointing, jeering, grabbing hold of Mick's arm as though only she had the right. Mick himself, taller by far, his dark hair curly where Debbie's was cut straight and short, watching her, expressionless.

She'd felt so good when he'd asked her to go out with him. Really nice-looking he was, better than anyone else she'd been with before. Two years older than her. In the sixth form. Always getting his name read out in assembly for scoring goals or something. He'd got his pick of the girls in the school, more or less. And he'd asked her.

'What you doing Saturday, Sharon?'

Leaning sideways against the wall in the corridor, half blocking her way. She hadn't even thought he'd known her name. Stood there blushing for all she was worth, she had, wondering if it were some kind of joke; hoping that it wasn't.

'Nothing.'

Staring at the floor, noticing how large his feet were and that he hadn't cleaned his shoes for ages.

'Come to the pictures then?'

Her scalp was on fire. 'Where?'

'Down the town. Meet you outside at half past seven. Right?'

'All right.'

Had she said it aloud or thought it? He'd nodded and walked away, leaving her there. Mr Dawson had come along the corridor behind her and waved his mark book in her direction. 'Come along, Sharon, keep your courting for out of school hours, if you please.'

And he'd waddled past smirking.

Sharon hadn't cared about old Dawson and his stupid remarks. She was going out with Mick Tracey and that was all that mattered. Mick Tracey!

All the form had been full of it, the girls anyway. Debbie and all her mates, even the snobby ones who lived in private houses in the Old Town had looked at her as if noticing her for the first time. Walking past the big Co-op windows on the way home, she had caught sight of someone attractive and only with difficulty recognized her own reflection.

'My, you are growing up pretty!' her nan had said the last time they'd gone down to London to visit her. But then her nan always said nice things.

When Sharon got home the day that Mick had asked her out, even her mother had noticed something unusual about her – and that was saying something.

Not that Sharon had told her, of course. Instead she had mumbled something about getting good marks for her maths.

'Not before time,' her mum had said, and carried on mixing the mashed potato.

And now ...

Sharon gripped the park bench tight. Tight. Tighter until the grain of it was hard against her hand. She pulled them away and looked at them, at the wavering lines across her skin.

And now he was going round with Debbie Bradley, and on Monday she would have to go into school and face them all.

*

'You took your time, madam.'

Sharon walked past her mother's back and set the shopping bag down on the kitchen table.

'Didn't you hear what I said?'

'Yes, Mum.'

'Why didn't you answer me then?'

Because it wasn't a question.

'Don't know, Mum.'

'Don't know, Mum,' her mother mocked. 'Well, all I can say is, it's a pity you don't. Swooning about all over the place. It's this new boy-friend of yours, isn't it?'

'I haven't got a new boy-friend.'

'Didn't go out by yourself last night, did you?'

Sharon carried on unpacking the things from the bag. Two packets of white sugar, half a pound of cheddar cheese, a pound of bacon, two packets of tea . . .

'Did you?' Her mother's voice was raised, her dark eyes staring at her daughter from under a brown fringe. Apart from being heavier, obviously older, Sharon and her mother were very similar in appearance. Without ever understanding why, Sharon sometimes thought that this was one of the reasons why her mother failed to like her very much.

'Well?'

'No, Mum.'

'He's your boy-friend then, isn't he?'

Having proved her point to her satisfaction, Sharon's mother turned her back and, with a nod of the head, began to wash some cups and saucers in the sink. Sharon finished getting the things out of the bag, folded it up and put it in a drawer, and tried to get out of the room unnoticed.

'Sharon?'

'Yes, Mum?'

'Make us a cup of tea, will you? I've been on the go ever since I got up, what with one thing and another. It's always the same, Saturdays your father's on shift. I wish he'd get a different job, I really do. One that would let him stay home more.'

Sharon turned on the tap. The sink was in front of the window and she looked out on to the narrow path that separated their front garden from the one opposite. An identical house staring back at theirs. She'd been seven when her father had taken his present job; since then she'd hardly seen him except at weekends – and then sometimes he did overtime. She had used to wish he would change his job, be at home more too. Now she was less certain : it was as though he had become almost a stranger to her.

'There's ever so many things want doing around the house,' her mother went on. 'He's been promising to put those new shelves up in the back for six months to my knowledge.' She sighed. 'Sharon, did you warm the pot before you put that tea in? How many times have I got to tell you? I don't know, really I don't.'

Sharon switched off the kettle; poured in the boiling water.

'Not that there's any chance of him changing his job now, not even if he wanted to. Lucky to have a job at all. There's more on social security round here than aren't.' She jabbed a finger at Sharon. 'You make sure you get them exams, my lady, or you'll end up on the dole like everyone else.'

Sharon poured the milk into the cups.

'D'you hear me, Sharon?'

'Yes, Mum.'

'That's all right, then. I only hope you prove it by getting those O-levels. Qualifications, that's what you need nowadays.'

Sharon set her cup down in the saucer. 'Mum, half the girls who left with O-levels last year haven't got jobs. Elizabeth Minehead's been out of work for ages and she got six. Lesley Jackson got five and she's working behind the cash desk in Woolie's. It doesn't make any difference, Mum. It's not worth all the fuss.'

There was a bang as a pan fell back on to the draining board. A finger was stuck half an inch away from Sharon's face.

'Don't you let me hear you say it's not worth the fuss! I don't want everyone gossiping about what a dunce you are. Mrs Atkinson was telling me her Lorraine expects to pass in ten subjects. Ten! If she can do it, then so can you.'

'Mum, that's not true. She's miles cleverer than I am.'

'Rubbish!'

Sharon sighed, picked up her cup and saucer and went to the door.

'Now where do you think you're going?'

'Upstairs. I've got homework to do.'

Sharon lay on her bed staring at the ceiling, at nothing. Downstairs she could hear her mother banging about in the kitchen, the way she always did whenever Sharon used her homework as an excuse to retreat to her own room. Trying to make her feel guilty.

Sharon sat up and stared at herself in the dressing-table mirror. That was typical! One minute her mum was going on about how important it was to work, and the next she was getting ratty about being left to do things herself.

Just as long as it suits her, thought Sharon, that's all that matters. She only wants me to pass so she's got something to brag about.

Even as the words formed, Sharon knew they weren't true.

Well, half true perhaps.

It wasn't as if her mum wanted her to have a career or anything like that. Not like Lorraine Atkinson who lived in a big house in the Old Town and whose mother managed the shop where Sharon's mum worked part-time. Lorraine was going to be a doctor, and had been ever since her parents had given her a nurse's outfit and a toy stethoscope at the age of five. A doctor, mind you, nothing as humble as a nurse.

Sharon's mum didn't see further than getting married at

twenty-two, moving into the council flat you've had your name down for since you were nineteen, and staying there for a couple more years until you started a family and moved into a corporation house.

A job was something you did to pass the time in between and to get a down payment on your three-piece suite. That was it. So what was the point of all the fuss.

Sharon got up and went to the window. The bedroom faced out over the back garden on to some garages. Behind the garages was an open concrete space, most of which she couldn't see. Then another row of houses identical to the one she lived in : kitchen downstairs at the front with a living-room behind it and a large hallway; two bedrooms and a bathroom upstairs.

Beyond the stacks of flat roofs, Sharon could see trees and the dark earth of fields. She leaned forward, face in her hands, elbows on the window ledge, looking out. Five, ten minutes.

'Sharon!' Her mother at the bottom of the stairs.

'Yes, Mum.'

'Are you getting on with your work?'

'Yes.'

'Are you sure?'

'Of course I am.'

'Just as long as you're not wasting your time daydreaming.'

Sharon didn't answer. After a few moments, her mother walked back into the kitchen.

Very slowly, Sharon gouged a deep line into the edge of the wood of the window-sill with her thumb nail. Then she went and sat on the bed, pulling a book from her bag and opening it. After five minutes she realized that she hadn't taken in a single word.

Sharon shut the book with a slap and threw it back on to the table. She wouldn't do it. Wouldn't! It was all stupid and silly and pointless. English and geography and needlecraft. She didn't care about passing exams and she didn't care what anyone said. Not the teachers, or her parents, or anyone. It was ...

She broke into a sudden sobbing, one hand sideways across her chest, the other to her face, trying to control the sound. The tears ran down her cheeks, along the forefinger of her right hand and on to her wrist, round under the arm and so on to her lap. The top of her body rocked slowly backwards and forwards; the noise grew louder, less controlled.

'Sharon! Sharon, what's going on up there?'

Footsteps on the stairs.

Sharon grabbed at a tissue from under her pillow and wiped it across her face, gasping.

'Sharon!'

Her mother's hand rattled the chrome handle of the door.

'Why is this door locked? Your father and I have told you before about doing that. Suppose you had an accident or something?'

Pause.

'Sharon, are you all right in there? Let me in.'

'I'm all right. Honestly. Nothing's the matter.'

'Of course something's the matter. I heard you crying.'

'I'm not crying.'

'But I heard you.'

'I banged my toe on the end of the bed. It's nothing. I'm working.'

Sharon sat white-faced, the green tissue screwed up and damp in her hand.

'What work?'

'An essay. For English. About this story we read.'

She could sense her mother moving away from the door, knew that she wanted to get back downstairs. When the footsteps had faded, Sharon went over to the dressing-table and sat down. She looked at her pale face, puffy eyes. Even her nan wouldn't say she was pretty now.

Tucked into the edge of the mirror were half of a cinema ticket and a torn cloakroom ticket from the Mecca.

2

Sharon waited alongside the bus lane. At that time of the morning the majority of buses were packed with people going to the industrial area beyond the railway station. She saw the double-decker she usually caught turn into the road past the Mecca, and then round and into the bus station.

She picked up her bag and stepped out of the queue. If she walked she'd be late, but she didn't care. At least she wouldn't have to put up with Debbie and her lot at registration. If she was lucky she could sneak into the back of Assembly before it was over. She could go to the office and make some excuse about being late and get her mark. Then it would be first lesson.

The school stood on the corner by a roundabout on one of the main roads out of town. Behind it, on two sides, were playing fields. Hockey goals, rugby posts – the soccer pitches were out of sight from where Sharon was walking. In the corner a high jump pit, the sand dirty and scattered with crisp bags.

Sharon walked past the side of the school quickly, not looking up at the dark green panels or the vast areas of glass for fear that someone should look out and recognize her.

She turned into the side road, heading for the entrance that was kept for the sixth form and the staff. She was less likely to get spotted that way.

Hurrying along, head down, she almost walked right into Mick Tracey. Her blue and white striped carrier-bag banged against his leg and she jumped, surprised.

'Watch it!'

He stood there, angry, looking at her. Black leather jacket, brown sweater, jeans; books in one hand.

'Sorry!' Sharon blurted out, wishing that she hadn't. 'I didn't see you.'

'No.'

A couple of other sixth formers went past, one of them making a remark Sharon didn't hear. Mick started to turn away.

Go on, thought Sharon, say something, say something!

'Mick . . .' It came out louder than she'd intended.

'Yea?'

'The other night. At the Mecca. I'm sorry. I . . .'

He shrugged his shoulders, looked round quickly to see if anyone else was watching.

'Don't matter, does it?'

He walked away quickly, going away from the main building towards the sixth-form block. Sharon stared after him, her bag swinging slightly from side to side.

Is that it, then? she'd wanted to ask. Are you going with Debbie Bradley now?

No. She was glad she hadn't said that, at least. Knew the answer; didn't want to hear him say it.

Sharon managed to keep out of Debbie's way until break. As soon as the bell went and they were dismissed, she almost ran out of the classroom and up to the dining area. Debbie and her mates wouldn't go up there. They'd be round by the bicycle sheds having a smoke.

Sharon bought a chocolate biscuit and a glass of orange and looked round. She saw Teresa Lane sitting at a table by herself and started to walk over towards her. Teresa was a strange girl, not quite like anyone else Sharon had ever met. Even her uniform, the grey skirt and red cardigan they were supposed to wear, never seemed to be the right shades. Not far enough out to get her told off; distinctive enough to stand out. And the way she spoke to the teachers, never rude, but, well, different – almost as if she were talking to them as equals.

'Hello, Teresa.'

''Lo, Sharon.'

'Want some of my biscuit?'

'No, thanks.'

Sharon nodded and had some of her drink. She still didn't know Teresa all that well. They'd never been in the same form and it was only since the fourth year they'd had any lessons together. They did the same art option that year and now they were in the same needlecraft group.

One thing she liked about Teresa, she stuck by herself. She never seemed to get involved in any gangs, just went her own way and talked to whoever she wanted to whenever she felt like it. No one ever acted stuck up with Teresa; they weren't catty to her either, not even behind her back.

Sharon thought the other girls were afraid of her.

When Teresa had been in the second year her mum had died. Sudden. She'd never been ill or anything; just went to bed one night and didn't wake up. Least, that was what Teresa had said.

Ever since then Teresa had more or less looked after the family. In the mornings she got the breakfast ready and made her dad's sandwiches for him to take to work. She took her younger brother, who was six, to the infant school before coming to school herself. She had permission to leave school ten minutes early so that she could collect him again and take him home and give him some tea.

After having something herself, she put her dad's tea in the oven and went off to do a couple of hours work as a cleaner on the industrial estate.

Somehow, in the middle of all that, she managed to have a steady boy-friend and to get some homework done.

Sharon didn't know how. She only found out about the boy-friend by accident. They'd been chatting about nothing in particular in needlecraft and Teresa had just come out with it. Sharon knew she hadn't seen her talking to boys in school much and had thought she wasn't interested; Teresa didn't go on about boys and sex all the time, the way the others did.

Anyway, his name was Laurence, although everyone called him Lol, even his parents. He was eighteen and was working as an apprentice carpenter. He had fair hair, almost as fair as Teresa's herself, and blue eyes that looked strange because of the way the bridge of his nose was twisted over to one side. When he was younger he'd fallen off some scaffolding and broken his nose and it had never straightened properly.

Lol met Teresa outside the school gates at lunchtime on Wednesdays, when he was on his way to the tech. He would turn his bike in small circles, occasionally revving the engine while he smoked a cigarette which he held cupped in his left hand.

Three or four evenings a week he went round to Teresa's house and watched telly, or played cards with her dad, while Teresa did her homework. Fridays and Saturdays they'd go up the pub with Lol's mates. Sundays he went round to Teresa's and had his dinner.

'Go anywhere this weekend?' Teresa asked.

'Mecca, Friday night.'

'Any good?'

Sharon could feel herself going red, tried to will herself to stop. 'All right, I suppose. Nothing special.'

'Go with anyone?'

Sharon pushed her hair away from her face with both hands and turned her head to one side. Debbie's mate, Janice, was standing by the wall across the dining-room, looking at them.

'Mick Tracey,' said Sharon so quietly that Teresa only just heard the name.

'Yea? You goin' with him, then?'

Sharon picked up her glass. 'Not really.'

They talked for a bit about Lol studying for his City and Guilds, then Teresa wandered off and Sharon thought she'd better go back to the loo before the bell went for break.

'Mrs Tabor's an old bag' someone had scrawled over the back of the door in large, angular letters. 'Are you sitting comfortably, then begin' was carved into the woodwork lower down. There was the usual collection of 'Tina 4 Keith' and 'Del 4 Me signed Me'. On the wall someone had done a drawing of Mr Williams in red felt tip : you could tell it was meant to be him because of his beard and those round, wire-framed glasses he wore.

On the floor were a few cigarette ends and some used matches.

Sharon pulled the chain and came out : they were standing by the wash basins.

''Ave a good time Sat'day night?'

Sharon wanted to push past them and get outside; she didn't; stood there, saying nothing. Debbie's short hair seemed to bristle on top; Carol leaned against the door, sneering.

'Good, was it, Sharon?'

'What?'

'Thought you was goin' with Mick Tracey Sat'day.'

'Yea. Letchworth to the pictures you told me.'

'What d'you see, Sharon?'

'Don't suppose she knows. Prob'ly didn't see much of the film.'

'No, her an' Mick up the back.'

'Dirty cow!'

Sharon blinked; saw herself reflected in the mirror between Heather and Janice. Pale, now. Biting her bottom lip.

Debbie slipped down from the wash basin where she had been sitting. 'Rotten, lyin' sod!'

Sharon twisted her head, felt cold in her stomach. 'What d'you mean? Who says I'm a liar?'

Debbie poked a finger at her. 'I do! You never went with Mick Sat'day night 'cause he was with me.'

'Yea!'

Alongside the reflection of her own face, Sharon could see Heather grinning, really enjoying it.

Sharon tried to get to the door, but Debbie pushed her back and Janice went and stood close behind her.

''E's not gonna waste 'is time goin' out with you, is 'e?'

'Wouldn't even let 'im 'ave an 'andful.'

'Tight cow!'

Sharon flailed at Debbie with her hand, missing her. Tears were running down her face.

'No, I'm not.'

'That's not what Mick says.'

'I don't believe you.'

They all stood there, laughing at her.

Carol moved her lanky body off the door. 'Having it off with 'im, then, are you?'

'Go on, Sharon, tell us what it's like.'

Debbie snorted. 'She don't know what it's like. Never 'ad it with anyone, 'ave you, Sharon?'

'Proper little virgin, in't you?'

'Miss high-an'-mighty!'

'Tight cow!'

Someone banged hard on the outside door : 'Come on, you girls, out of there. The bell's gone ages ago.'

Muffled giggling, shuffling of feet. Another bang. Louder this time. 'Come on! Off to lessons. I shall wait here until you come out.'

'Ooh, Mr Fletcher,' called Carol, 'I never knew you cared.'

They swept out, laughing and pushing, and went noisily down the corridor. Sharon stayed where she was, wiping the tears from her face with her hand, looking at herself in the mirror. After a few moments she went back into the cubicle and locked the door.

It was too late to go to her lesson; she would have to make up some excuse if anyone noticed she was missing. Sharon turned the corner thinking she might go to the library and try to spend the time till the bell in there.

One of the junior classes was inside: boys and girls pretending an interest in the shelves between playing chase round the stacks of books; gossiping in huddles; looking up what they thought were dirty words in the dictionaries.

'What do you want?' The librarian was plump, bespectacled; she wore a tabard made of coarse woven material with a brightly coloured pattern.

'A book, Miss.'

'What sort of book? What topic?'

Sharon began to blush and push at her brown hair. She ummed and fluttered.

'Who sent you?'

Sharon sucked in her lips, from nowhere feeling her head begin to ache, tears starting to prick at the back of her eyes.

'Whose class are you in this lesson?'

'Mrs Evans, Miss.'

One of the boys tripped over a chair and went sprawling; the class teacher shouted at him and the shout was lost in the uproar.

'May I remind you that there is a rule of silence in this library!' the librarian had yelled almost directly into Sharon's ear and when she turned back to Sharon her cheeks were bright red.

'Well, what did Mrs Evans send you to look up?' she snapped.

Sharon turned and ran, nearly knocking into an older girl coming through the door, her arms laden with books and files. By the time she was at the end of the corridor, the tears were streaming down her face and it was all that she could do to see where she was going. Finally, she came to a halt in one of the cloakrooms and sat on a bench alongside the wall.

Damp tissue screwed up in her hand, she sat there, aching, wanting to be anywhere but where she was and not knowing where else she wanted to be.

'Hello.'

Sharon jerked upright, sniffed.

'Are you all right?'

It was the sixth former she had almost collided with rushing out of the library. Now, Sharon realized that she recognized her; the girl had been one of their form prefects for a term of the previous year.

'Aren't you feeling well?'

'I'm all right.'

'Miss Parsons asked me to come and see where you'd got to. She said when she asked you what you were doing in the library you seemed upset. You nearly sent me flying.'

Sharon shuffled her feet, pushed at her nose with the fraying tissue.

'Here.'

The prefect handed her a clean, white tissue. Sharon hesitated, then took it, wiping the corners of her eyes and her cheeks, finally blowing her nose.

'Thanks.' She held out her hand as if offering the tissue back.

'You keep it. Do you want another one – I've got plenty.'

'It's okay.'

Sharon remembered her name now : Alison Westford. At least she wasn't bossy like some of them; didn't shout either. Sharon looked at her. She wasn't wearing jeans and fancy tops like most of the sixth form, just a grey skirt that didn't have a lot of shape to it and a blue jumper. Her hair was tidy and nothing more and she wasn't wearing any make-up. Sharon thought she seemed really grown-up, years and years older than she was herself.

'Whose lesson should you be in?'

'Evans.'

'Why are you skipping it then?'

'I'm not, I . . .'

Alison shook her head. 'Calm down, it's none of my business. I only wondered if I could do anything. Help.'

'No.' Sharon looked up at Alison again, then away. 'No, thanks.'

'You're in that Debbie Bradley's class, aren't you?'

Sharon nodded.

'Can't stand that girl. She hasn't been getting at you, has she?'

Sharon said, 'No,' very quietly.

Alison hesitated, then : 'Do you want to talk about it?'

Sharon looked away, shook her head.

'Okay, then. I'll tell Miss Parsons you're all right. 'Bye.'

The prefect went back towards the library, leaving Sharon alone with the rows of coats and herself.

'Miss Keble, I wonder if I might have a word?'

Seconds after the final bell : the form would be on their way back from the maths block. Mrs Evans shut the door behind her and set her smile in place.

'It's about Sharon Holmes.'

'Sharon? What's she been up to?'

'It's what she hasn't been up to that concerns me.'

Miss Keble managed to avoid sighing. She sat down behind her desk, waited.

'She didn't come to my lesson this morning. After break.' Mrs Evans brushed an imaginary cotton from her plaid skirt. 'She was in school this morning?' Knowing the answer.

'Yes. Yes, I'll speak with her. I'm sure there was some reason, she ...'

'There always is, isn't there?'

Miss Keble stood up. Mrs Evans readjusted her smile.

'You will be sure she comes to me and makes her apologies?'

'Of course.'

At the door, the older teacher turned. Voices from outside. 'I wonder if you could find out why Sharon hasn't handed in any homework for the last two weeks?'

She opened the door and stood quite still until those milling round waiting to collect their things had grudgingly made space for her to pass through.

The class erupted round Miss Keble; shrieks and banging of desks, threats and the occasional, 'Good night, Miss'. Eager for distance.

'Sharon. Sharon Holmes.'

Sharon stopped, stranded half way between her desk and the door. The others hurried past her, not wanting Miss Keble to find an excuse for keeping them back.

'You haven't got a school bus to catch, have you?'

'No, Miss.'

The last remaining boy was tugging a track suit top from underneath the jumbled mass of books inside his desk. It came out with a flourish, fetching several of the books with it.

'If that desk of yours wasn't in such a state, Neil, you wouldn't have that difficulty.'

'No, Miss.' Throwing the books back and letting the lid fall with a bang. 'Night, Miss.'

Miss Keble waited for the classroom door to slam also, put her hands to her ears and made an exaggerated grimace, then smiled at Sharon reassuringly.

Sharon didn't looked reassured.

'Sit down, then. I wanted to talk to you.'

Sharon wavered, bag in one hand. 'I can't stay long, I ...'

'It's all right. I shan't keep you.'

Sharon sat down. Miss Keble was all right really. At least she didn't get on at you the way some of the others did. Tried to be fair – though with kids like Debbie and Heather, God knows how she kept her patience sometimes.

'Mrs Evans says you weren't in her lesson this morning.'

Sharon blinked : 'When was that, Miss?'

'After break.'

'Oh.'

'Oh.'

Sharon shifted on her chair, pushed her fingers together, stared at them.

'Is that right?'

'Don't know, Miss,' pressing her hands together harder, the skin around the knuckles turning white.

'Now that won't do, will it? You must know where you were.'

'After break?'

'Yes.'

'I was ... I was in the loo, Miss. The toilet.'

'All lesson?'

'Yes, Miss. Nearly.'

Miss Keble moved some papers around on her desk and looked at Sharon doubtfully.

'I came on this morning,' Sharon said quickly. 'It was hurting me.'

'And that's why you were late for school, I suppose?'

Sharon grasped at it: 'Yes, Miss.'

'You know you're supposed to go to the sick room, don't you?'

Sharon nodded.

Miss Keble sighed. 'All right, I'll see Mrs Evans. But you'll have to see her as well.'

'Oh, do I, Miss?'

'Yes, Sharon, you do.' Firmer now. 'You can go and see her at registration in the morning. And just make sure you're here for registration. All right?'

'Yes, Miss Keble.'

Sharon stood up and pushed at the falling piece of hair. She got hold of her bag and lifted it off the top of the other desk.

'Mrs Evans also said you haven't been getting your homework in on time.'

Sharon took a couple of paces towards the door.

Miss Keble pushed her chair round, picked up the papers again and straightened them.

'You know we're doing reports at the moment, don't you? There's a lot of comments about you not getting work in, skipping it altogether. Have you done my English for the week, for instance?'

Sharon looked down at her bag.

'Oh, Sharon, really. How do you expect to pass your exams this way?'

No response.

'Well?'

'I don't know, Miss. I'll do the essay tonight. Honest.'

Miss Keble stood up. 'By rights I should tell Mrs Tabor. As head of the year, she'll send a letter home.'

'Oh, no, Miss. Don't do that!'

'That's up to you, isn't it?'

'It's my mum. She's not very well. It would really upset her, getting a letter from the school. I'll do the essay. I'll give it to you tomorrow.'

'And the other work?'

'Yes, Miss. I'll catch up, I promise. I've had to help at home, you see, with me mum not being so well.'

'All right, then, Sharon. This time. But I want to see that essay on "The Machine Stops" on my desk first thing in the morning.'

Sharon was already by the door.

'And Sharon?'

Her head turned back into the room.

'Don't forget you've got to see Mrs Evans.'

Sharon shut the door behind her. Miss Keble looked round the room. Six chairs left unstacked. One window still to close. A pile of sweet papers on the floor under the desks at the back. Someone's coat left in a heap. 'Spurs are the Greatest' scrawled on the board, the letters sloping upwards and getting bigger and bigger.

She shook her head and began to tidy up before the cleaners came in.

Sharon hesitated in the corridor : she didn't want to bump into Debbie's lot again and it was possible they were hanging around waiting for her. Down the corridor, a group of fifth-year boys barged their way into the room where detentions were held. Two girls from lower down the school went past her carrying hockey sticks.

Sharon decided to go round the other way. She was less than ten yards into the lower playground when she stopped dead.

In huge chalk letters on the brickwork at the foot of the sixth-form block, someone had written:

'OH, NO'

says

SHARON

She stood and stared at it, unable to believe that it was really there.

They couldn't have! They couldn't have!

She heard footsteps coming along behind her and started to run. Half way across the playground, the handles of her carrier-bag came away and everything scattered all over the concrete.

3

The next morning Sharon complained that she was feeling sick and had a headache. For once her mother hardly argued; she could have the day off school.

Sharon wrote a side and a half of file-paper about what picture of society in the future is painted in 'The Machine Stops', and how much room for hope does it leave? A third of the essay was taken up with two long quotations. She made a list of raising agents and their principal uses, as well as attempting an exercise on simultaneous equations. This she gave up after number four.

On the Wednesday she returned to school with two notes. One for the form teacher to explain her absence and the other for the P.E. teacher asking that she be excused from games.

For the rest of that week Sharon did her best to keep out of Debbie Bradley's way and for her part Debbie didn't seem to mind. She was too full of what was going on between Mick Tracey and herself to be bothered with the likes of Sharon.

The chalked writing had been washed off the sixth-form wall and no one mentioned it at all. Sharon kept wondering whether Mick had seen it and, if so, what he'd thought.

Apart from during Assembly, when he sat rather self-consciously with the rest of the Upper Sixth at the back of the stage, she only saw him once. In the middle-distance, wearing his soccer gear and punting a ball ahead of him.

On the Friday Debbie was away herself: so was Janice. They usually truanted together.

Nor was their reason hard to find. Friday was the day for giving out reports.

The class had already addressed their own envelopes and

at the end of the day, Miss Keble handed them back with the reports inside.

'One thing. Let me remind you that there's a parents' evening for all of the fifth year on Monday evening. Your parents have already had a circular about that, but please will you remind them. Seven o'clock in the hall.'

Shuffling of feet, fidgeting with envelopes.

'May I also remind you that now you are regarded as being responsible young people ...' Groans all round. '... you are also invited to attend and hear what we've got to say about you. Oh, and one last thing, remember those reports are addressed to your parents and intended for them. Not you.'

The class pushed for the door, suddenly talking very loudly and knocking some of the desks sideways. Two of the boys had slit the ends of their envelopes before they were outside the classroom.

When Sharon got home, her mum was sitting in the living-room with the curtains pulled half closed, watching television. Through the other part of the window, Sharon could see the double line of washing.

'Mum, I don't want any tea yet. I'm going up to my room to get some homework done first.'

Her mother scarcely glanced up. 'All right, love.'

As soon as she was upstairs, Sharon fished out the envelope from between the pages of the exercise book where she had put it to stop it getting creased.

She sat on the end of the bed and looked at her own neat but uninteresting handwriting. It was addressed to Mr and Mrs J. Holmes. Sharon felt the folded paper inside and dreaded knowing what was written on it. She remembered the look that had been on Miss Keble's face when she'd handed it to her. A sort of half-smile that said, don't take it too badly.

Sharon had never opened one of her reports before. She

knew that most of the others did, but her parents had always made a point of showing her so she'd never thought it was worth the risk. If they found out, she knew they'd be angry.

And as a rule her reports weren't all that dreadful. Nothing, really. Remarks like could try harder or average effort. They didn't get form positions any more so it was difficult for her parents to get a clear idea of what was going on. They always said they were going to the parents' evenings, but only rarely did they actually turn up. There was usually something else to do. Or her dad was working late and her mum refused to go on her own.

But this time ...

She looked at the flap; it had been stuck down hard. Sharon tried pushing one finger under the edge, but it wouldn't go. What she should do was take it downstairs and steam it open, she knew that. But if she did her mum was sure to ask her what she was doing, or walk in and catch her.

The tip of her finger had worked a small gap right at the end of the envelope. She pushed right and left, enlarging the space, lifting the gummed section of brown paper. She was biting down on the fleshy inside of her bottom lip and holding her breath.

Let it open cleanly!

Below, she was aware of the television sound being turned off; she waited, finger inside the envelope. Her mother turned on the tap to fill the kettle; she was going to make the tea.

Sharon pushed the finger further – the top crease of the envelope ripped across and down.

Sharon closed her eyes for a second, breathing deeply. Then she stared at it closely: the tear came down a good inch. There was no way in which she was ever going to be able to reseal it so that her parents wouldn't notice. No way at all.

She ripped the rest of the opening quickly across and pulled out the folded report. She listened to the sounds of her mother in the kitchen, moved instinctively round so that her back was to the door, and opened it out.

Sharon shook a little as she read. The first time her eyes raced over the lines, searching for something good, something reassuring. Then back, slowly, feeding it all in. A third time and a fourth.

It wasn't fair. It just wasn't fair!

Apart from D.S. there wasn't a single good remark. And even she said 'modestly' – whatever that meant. Sharon's eyes went up and down through the columns. 'A consistently weak performance.' That mean sod, Dawson, standing there doing stupid things with his mouth to show them how to pronounce words properly. If only he knew how daft he looked! Like a fat goldfish in a bowl. A fat French goldfish, puckering his lips and rolling his eyes. And he was sarcastic! Picking her up every time she said something wrong, making a joke of it, encouraging the others to laugh at her. His little pets! What was the point of learning French anyway? She wasn't ever going to go there. Not even for a holiday.

And as for Williams – he was another one who was sarcastic all the time. It shouldn't be allowed. Teachers shouldn't be allowed to make remarks like that. If you ever tried it back on them, they soon lost their tempers. But you. Oh, no, you had to sit there and take it.

'Little has been attempted, less achieved.' That was typical of him. Really typical. It wasn't as if he ever did anything himself. Stuck a few daft objects on a table and told everyone to draw them. Or put some horrid, loud rock record on and told them to paint whatever came into their heads. Nothing came into hers, not ever. Anyway, he only did it because he wanted everyone to think how with-it he was.

Sharon stood up and went to the window. Someone in one of the houses at the other side of the garages was putting up new curtains in one of their bedroom windows. They were lime green with black squiggly patterns running down them.

In the distance, outside the town, it looked as if it was raining.

Sharon sat back on the bed. She'd thought Miss Keble would have tried to say something nice, at least. She worked hard; she did her best. Well, some of the time. But sometimes she just didn't understand. All that Shakespeare. How were they supposed to make sense of it when half the words were funny? What was the point of reading some old play written hundreds of years ago, anyway? Why didn't they do something modern? Up-to-date.

In the C.S.E. group they had things like 'To Sir, With Love' and that 'Kes' to read. She wouldn't mind having to do those. One lunchtime she'd picked up one of those 'Kes' books with the picture on the front of that boy sticking two fingers up and started to read it. She'd finished two chapters by the end of lunch and it had been really interesting.

Better than the stuff they had for O-level.

Behind Sharon the bedroom door opened. Her heart leaped and she turned round and there was her mother, standing with a cup of tea in her left hand. Standing there with her back arched and her eyes fixed on the piece of paper in Sharon's hand.

'Forgot to lock it this time, didn't you, madam?'

Sharon looked at her mother in the doorway, feeling helpless, helpless and sick.

'I thought you'd like a nice cup of tea while you were doing your work.' Her voice was icy, hard.

The report dangled uselessly from Sharon's hand.

'You'd better give that to me.'

Sharon held it up towards her mother, trying to look the other way.

'Give it here, then. Don't expect me to come and get it.'

Sharon pushed herself up off the bed. When she got close to her mother and saw her eyes she was afraid. For a moment she thought she was going to be hit.

Sharon flinched.

Mrs Holmes took the report and turned round without another word. She walked downstairs, taking the cup of tea with her.

Sharon stayed in her room, the door closed but not locked. She made no attempt to go down for tea, neither did her mother call her. She switched on her small transistor radio and listened to Capital for a few minutes. She switched it off again and began to doodle on the front of a school exercise book.

At half past five she heard her father come in. Bracing herself for his voice summoning her or his arrival outside her room, all that she heard were voices talking urgently and then, after five minutes or so, the television going on.

Her father always liked to watch the news.

At six o'clock, the sound went off again.

Sharon broke the point of her pencil against the book cover. She half thought she would go downstairs and have it out with them. Keeping her waiting like that.

'Sharon!'

She opened the door slowly and stepped outside. At the bottom of the brown stair carpet, her father stood tapping his left hand impatiently against his leg.

'Come down here.'

She tried not to look at his grey eyes, unusually stern. He'd changed out of his work clothes into a pair of shapeless brown trousers and the same chunky green cardigan he always wore around the house.

'Come in here.'

He stood by the living-room door and ushered Sharon past him. Her mother was sitting in her armchair on the far side of the fire. She was wearing her glasses, the ones she used for reading. Her face looked strained, tense.

'Sit down.'

Sharon went over and sat on the settee, tucking one leg behind the other and pulling her skirt down at the hem. Her father looked at her for a few moments, without speaking. Then he sat in the chair on the other side of the fire.

The front of the fire was switched on, so that the orange light glowed and the metal fan behind it turned, giving a flickering effect. Neither of the bars was on.

The living-room door was ajar.

On the low coffee-table, in the middle of the room, lay the report. The two ends, where it had been folded, pushed upwards : it looked like a stranded bird.

'Well?'

Sharon blinked at her father and shook her head once, not meaning anything.

'Tell your father what you've done.'

Mr Holmes looked across the table at his wife quickly, as though annoyed that she'd interrupted. 'Well, Sharon, I'm waiting,' he said.

Sharon sniffed. 'What for?'

'Don't answer your father back!'

'Maureen, don't ...'

'What d'you want me to say? You know what I did. You can see. What's the point of me saying it?'

Sharon was leaning forward, staring at her father.

'Jack, don't let her ...'

'That's right, you let her tell you what to do. Just like ...'

He jumped from his chair and slapped her round the face. Sharon fell backwards, then sideways, both hands to her cheek, the tears smarting in her eyes.

'Jack! You shouldn't have!'

'Shut up, Maureen! For God's sake, shut up!'

Still crying, Sharon heard her mother hurry out of the room, shutting the door with a bang. She knew her father was standing over her and she kept her face hidden inside her hands, sobbing and shaking. Her cheek was stinging and she was breathing unevenly.

'Sharon.'

She could sense him leaning over her and when he put his

hand on her shoulder she flinched. He pulled the hand away quickly and moved back to the fire.

'I lost my temper. I'm sorry.'

Sharon sat up a little more, still not looking round. She rubbed at her eyes, reaching under the sleeve of her jumper for a crumpled tissue.

'Come on, Sharon, it wasn't that hard.'

She turned and looked up at him. No, it hadn't been that hard. It had been the shock, the surprise. He hadn't hit her since she was a little girl and she'd lied about stealing sweets from a jar in the kitchen. She'd been seven and afterwards he'd picked her up and held her in his arms and cuddled her.

While they were like that, her mother came back into the room. She was smoking, a thing she rarely did, and her mouth was drawn in tightly. She stepped between them and sat back in her chair without looking at either of them.

Somewhere outside a dog barked.

'Why did you do it, Sharon?'

'I didn't think it mattered. All of the other kids open theirs.'

'That's not an answer, is it?'

'She did it because she was ashamed of what was in it.' Her mother's voice was bitter, edgy.

'If I was ashamed of it, what would I want to look at it for?'

'Don't you raise your voice to me, young lady, or I'll get your father to give you another backhander!'

'Yes, you would!'

They were both standing, leaning slightly forwards, eyes bright. Mr Holmes stepped past the table and took hold of his wife by the shoulders.

'Maureen, that won't do any good.'

'Won't it? Perhaps if you'd done it more often she wouldn't be in the mess she is now.'

'I'm not in a mess,' Sharon shouted defiantly.

Her father ignored her, shaking his head, his hands still on his wife's shoulders.

'Maureen.'

'What?' she snapped.

'All that won't help now.'

She shot him a fierce glance : 'No, it won't, will it?'

She shook herself free and sat down heavily, knocking her glasses from the arm of the chair on to the carpet. He bent down and picked them up, replacing them.

'I'll make some tea,' he said.

All the while he was in the kitchen, Sharon and her mother didn't look at one another. Mrs Holmes smoked another cigarette and Sharon watched the movements of the electric fire.

When they'd all started their first cup, Mr Holmes reached down and picked up the report. He looked at it and set it down on his lap.

'All right, Sharon, we'll forget the fact that you opened it when you shouldn't have.'

'No, we ...'

'We'll forget all about that. But what about the report itself?'

Sharon put her cup down in the saucer, rattling it against the spoon. She didn't know what to say.

'I mean,' her father went on, 'it isn't very good, is it?'

'Not very good!' said her mother quickly. 'It's awful!'

He looked across at her. 'Now, Maureen, it's not that bad.'

'Well, I don't see how it could be much worse.'

Sharon sighed and they both looked at her.

'Why haven't you been working?' her father asked.

'I have.'

'Not according to this, you haven't.'

'Oh, teachers are never satisfied.'

'But you've got such low grades. There isn't anything over a C.'

'C's average.'

'Well, you're better than average.'

'They don't think so.'

'When you were at junior school,' Mrs Holmes said, 'you were always coming top in things. You used to get ever such good reports. You got a prize once.'

'It wasn't a prize, Mum, it was a book for helping in the library.'

'That's beside the point, Sharon,' said her father. 'What I want to know is why everyone says you could have done better.'

'Because they always say that.'

'Not if they don't mean it.'

'And what about your exams?' asked her mother sharply. 'It doesn't sound as if you're going to pass anything.'

Sharon opened her mouth to say something but thought better of it. Her mother got up and took the report from her husband's lap. She sat down with it and put on her glasses.

Mr Holmes glanced quickly at Sharon, then poured out some more tea.

'You see what the headmaster says ...' her mother began.

'What does he know about it?'

Mrs Holmes slapped the report against her knee. 'That only goes to show what an ignorant little madam you are.'

'He doesn't even know who I am.'

'Of course he does. What do you think he's paid for?'

'Oh, Mum!'

Mrs Holmes glanced at the report again. 'What about Mrs Keble, then?'

'Miss.'

'Miss Keble, whatever she is. She knows you well enough, I suppose?'

Sharon shrugged her shoulders.

'See what she says – "disappointing".' She tapped the paper with her other hand. ' "Preoccupied with other things". What have you got to say about that?'

'Nothing.'

'What sort of other things, Sharon?' asked her father.

'I don't know, Dad.' Voice rising again. 'I didn't write it, did I? You'd better ask her.'

As soon as the words were out of her mouth, Sharon wanted to swallow them back. But her father carried on as though she hadn't said it.

'Well, what have you been thinking about when you should have been paying attention to your work?'

'I told you, I don't . . .'

'It's that boy, that's who it is,' interrupted her mother with a note almost of triumph.

'What boy?'

'Which boy is this, Sharon?'

'The boy she's been going out with.'

'Which boy, Sharon?'

Sharon pointed over at her mother. 'Ask her. She knows more about it than I do.'

Mrs Holmes jutted a hand in Sharon's direction. 'I will not have you talking to me like that! Is that clear?'

'Yes, Mum.' Almost too softly to be heard.

The arm jerked again. 'Is it?'

'Yes, Mum.'

Her father put down his cup and saucer. 'Sharon, who is this boy?'

Sharon looked at him wildly. 'There isn't any boy! There isn't any boy!' She screamed and hugged her knees up to her chest, burying her face between them.

'That's it,' said her mother. 'You cry. Get your father feeling sorry for you again.'

Sharon pulled her head away and glared: 'I'm not crying. I'm not . . . I'm not . . .'

She continued to stare at her mother, tears trickling from the corners of her eyes.

'Your mother only wanted to know who you've been seeing. If you've . . . if you're . . . involved in some way that's taking your mind off your work, we want to know about it, that's all.'

'Dad, there isn't any boy. I'm not going out with anybody.'

'You were, though, weren't you?' said Mrs Holmes.

'Yes! All right, yes, I was going out with someone and I'm not any more.'

'And who was he? Someone from school?'

Sharon sat forward onto the edge of the settee, then collapsed back again. 'Yes,' she answered quietly. 'His name's Mick Tracey and he's in the sixth form.'

Her mother's eyes flickered across the room. 'In that case, he ought to know better. I've a good mind to write a letter to the headmaster.'

'You can't!' Sharon was on her feet and shouting. 'You can't! Everyone'll laugh at me. You can't do that.' She pulled at her hair and twisted her head to one side. 'It doesn't ... there isn't ... I'm not going with him any more. I'm not, honest I'm not.'

Sharon stood there in the middle of the room, suddenly self-conscious.

Her mother grunted and opened the packet of cigarettes.

'All right,' her father said, 'no one's going to write a letter.'

Sharon crossed her arms, holding herself. Her mother struck a match and the flame startled upwards.

'I'm going upstairs,' said Sharon and left the room. Neither of her parents said anything.

There was a cat on the garage roof, grey and white, sitting on the corner like a statue. Sharon bit the inside of her lip. What right had they to go on at her like that? Moaning on and on, asking her questions as though it was some kind of interrogation. And ... she put her hand to her face where her father had struck her. If only she lived with someone nice like her nan ...

At half past eight there was a quiet knock on the door and Sharon's father came in with a tray. There was a mug of coffee and some ham sandwiches. He set down the tray on the table.

'Thanks, Dad.'

His face looked drawn, his eyes tired; a shadow of stubble darkened his chin. He looked back into the room from the door. 'This parents' evening on Monday. You'd better come with us.'

The Valley Comprehensive School

Report for the half year ending 28th February 1977

Name **Sharon Holmes** Form **5 TK** Age **15:6** Average Age **16:2**
Absences **8** Times Late **14**

Subject	Effort	Grade	Comment	
English	c	D+	Sharon has some ability, but must work much harder if she is to pass 'O' level	M.K
Mathematics	D	D	Sharon makes little effort, and her work shows only a poor understanding	GE
French	D	E	A consistently weak performance	CD.
German				
History				
Geography	C+	C	Sharon has done some quite good work	K
Biology	c	c	Fair progress	M.D
Physics or Chemistry	D	D	Sharon does not show any interest	PR
Religious Education	C	C	Rather disappointing.	TL.
Woodwork or Domestic Science	C+	C+	Good. Sharon has continued to work modestly but well.	AMcL
Metalwork or Needlecraft	D	D	Untidy and disorganized	RE
Art	D	C	Little has been attempted, less achieved	AW
Physical Education	c	c	Fair	H

Really this is a disappointing report. I had hoped that Sharon
would appreciate the importance of this year's work and
make a greater effort, but this has not been the case. Too often
her mind seems preoccupied with other things. Form Teacher **M. Keble**

Sharon is allowing important educational opportunities
to pass her by. She must make a determined effort
before it is too late.

Headmaster **K J Leman**

4

Sharon woke up early: the milkman was clunking bottles somewhere at the back and the sun angled in between the drawn curtains. She looked at the little clock on her table: a quarter to seven. No one else would be up. She pushed back the bedclothes and swung round, feet pushing into her blue and cream slippers – a present from her nan last Christmas.

She went quietly to the bathroom; came back and changed out of her pyjamas into her school things; sprawled across the end of the bed and opened the book of poetry she'd been told to read for homework. Some stuff by Blake that they'd looked at last term. Read the poems through and be prepared to talk about them, Miss Keble had said. If there are things you don't understand, make a note of them and ask me in class.

Sharon turned the pages, flicking from one to another, reading one line here, a couple more further on. She could hear the traffic building up on the road into the town; someone was moving around downstairs. The tap spurted on, then off.

> Can I see a falling tear,
> And not feel my sorrow's share?
> Can a father see his child
> Weep, nor be with sorrow fill'd?

Sharon shut the book and put it in her bag, together with the other things she needed. Tucked into her maths exercise book was the reply slip signed to say that her parents would be attending the parents' meeting that evening.

Some of the bedroom curtains in the row opposite were still drawn. The sun reflected off the edges of the roofs. She thought she'd walk to school for a change.

She turned left outside the house and walked up the path towards the square at the top. As she cut across, a tabby cat with a white front and a red collar miaowed at her from the low wall that went round a clump of bushes in the middle of the square.

Sharon stopped and bent to stroke it. The cat turned its back towards her, head arched. She scratched it above the tail and it moved round to face her, purring.

After a few moments, she patted it and walked on. When she turned at the far side, the cat was sitting on the corner of the wall, looking at her.

Sharon went down the underpass and on to the path that led towards the lakes. There were already children playing outside the junior school away to the left. It didn't matter; she'd given herself plenty of time.

She was almost by the first lake – the one with the ducks – when she saw Teresa Lane coming round from the other direction, walking with her little brother. Sharon waited so that they would meet up with her.

'Didn't know you came this way?'

'Don't as a rule. Usually get the bus.'

'S'almost as quick cuttin' through. Saves money.'

'S'pose it does.'

They went past the yard where all the boats were kept; yachts with their masts sticking up at odd angles; flat boats covered by tarpaulin. As they walked round the back of the café, a brown alsatian came up to them, showing his teeth and growling quietly. Sharon stopped, holding her bag in front of her.

''E won't hurt you,' said Teresa. 'Not if you ignore 'im.'

She went on, pulling her brother by the hand. Sharon followed, not daring to look at the dog, frightened that it might jump at her from behind.

'You're not frightened of dogs, are you?'

'Those I am. They killed a boy not long ago. I read it in the paper. Bit his throat.'

The little boy gazed up at Sharon in horror. The sunlight was reflecting off the surface of the water, making it sparkle.

'Your dad going to the parents' meeting?' Sharon asked.

'You're jokin'!'

They had to leave the path and cut through some trees to get to the road.

'Why? 'S yours?'

'Yes. Me mum and dad.'

'You goin', too?'

'Yea. Don't want to, though.'

'Why you goin', then?'

'Me dad says I've got to. 'S about my report.'

Teresa laughed. 'Rotten, was it?'

'Me mum and dad thought it was. You should 'ave heard them getting on at me about it. Specially me mum. Really miserable to me, my mum is sometimes.'

Sharon stopped talking, looking at Teresa and her brother. A few minutes later, Teresa went left towards her brother's school and Sharon carried on alone.

Teresa sat at the table by the window, copying up somebody's biology notes. In the middle of the room, Lol and her dad were playing draughts. Teresa heard her brother coughing upstairs; laid down her pen. After a few moments he stopped and she went back to her work.

'You ain't thinkin', Lol.'

'Who says I ain't?'

'I do.'

Mr Lane hopped his king over Lol's last three pieces and sat back with a grin.

'Beaten you again, 'as he?' Teresa asked.

'Luck, i'nit?'

Teresa's dad stood up and hitched up his trousers. 'That's not luck, old son. That's judgement. Skill and judgement, that's what that is.'

'Huh!' Lol started putting the pieces back in the box. 'I'm off out, then.'

Teresa looked at him : 'Oh, remembered the parents' evening up at the school, have you?'

'Come off it. I'm goin' up the pub. Promised I'd meet this bloke, didn't I?'

'Oh, yes?' Teresa looked across at Lol, who winked.

'Shan't be long,' putting on his coat. 'Take it easy, you two. Remember what I say . . .'

'We know . . .' Teresa began.

'. . . don't do anything you wouldn't do,' they chorused.

Mr Lane went out.

Lol switched on the television and watched it for a few minutes, then switched it off again; picked up the paper, put it down.

'What you doin'?'

'Biology.'

Lol leaned over the back of the settee : 'Come over 'ere, then. I'm good at biology.'

'Yea, an' we all know what sort.'

Lol grinned : after writing another sentence, Teresa went over to him.

It wasn't until a quarter to nine that Sharon's parents finally got to see Miss Keble. By that time Mrs Holmes was scarcely speaking and her expression seemed to have frozen on to her face. Sharon's dad had been asking a few questions, nodding, staring down at the report. Sharon could tell that he felt really awkward, out of place.

For herself, she was hardly ever referred to directly : it was as if she weren't there at all.

Miss Keble looked up from her list and smiled at Sharon. She stood up and held out her hand to her father, then her mother.

'You must be Mr and Mrs Holmes?'

Nods. Smiles, somewhat uncertain.

'I expect you're feeling quite tired by now. You must have seen a lot of teachers already?'

Mr Holmes nodded again.

'Please sit down. You, too, Sharon.'

Miss Keble placed a tick alongside Sharon's name.

'I don't think we've met before.'

'Er, no, it's, well it's not always . . .'

'I'm afraid it hasn't always been convenient. My husband works on shift, you see, and . . .'

'Yes, of course. I quite understand. But now, what would you like to know?'

Sharon's parents exchanged a hasty glance.

'How she's getting on, I suppose,' her father said.

Miss Keble drew breath. 'Well, you've seen the report.'

'Yes.' Mr Holmes opened it on the table and looked at it again.

'It's bad, isn't it?' her mother said.

Miss Keble gestured vaguely with her right hand, biro between two fingers. 'It certainly isn't good. As they've probably told you tonight, most people who teach Sharon seem to think she could have been working far harder.'

'Yes, well, we've told her, haven't we, Jack. We're always telling her.'

'What about you, Sharon?' said the teacher. 'Do you think you could have been working harder?'

'Sometimes, Miss.' Fidgeting. 'I do try, though.'

'Do sit still, Sharon. Stop wriggling around.'

Sharon pulled at her hair and looked down the long room. Lorraine Atkinson and her mother were standing with Mr Williams, all three of them laughing. Lorraine was wearing a long dress in a blue flowery print and her hair was held by a black velvet ribbon. Sharon thought she looked as though she ought to be at a dance rather than a parents' evening.

'What about her English?' asked Mr Holmes. 'What chance has she got of passing her O-levels?'

'That depends on how much revision she does, of course, but . . .' Miss Keble ran her fingers along a line in her mark book. 'I'm afraid the marks Sharon got in the mocks aren't very promising. She . . .'

'But she's always been good at English,' Mrs Holmes interrupted. 'Reading and spelling. At the juniors . . .'

Miss Keble sighed and raised both hands. 'Studying for O-level isn't quite the same, Mrs Holmes.' She looked across at the father. 'Sharon has a great deal of trouble understanding the literature work. Especially the Shakespeare. Unless she gets down to it really hard, I think her chances of passing are very slight.'

'English is so important, though, isn't it? I mean, if she leaves without her English what chance has she got of getting a decent job?'

'She might pass the language, of course,' said Miss Keble. 'If she can pick up another ten, no, fifteen per cent on her mock then she'd be in with a chance.'

Mr Holmes looked at his wife and smiled. 'Oh, well, that's good to hear, at least. You can work hard and make that up, can't you, Sharon?'

Sharon was sitting with her back half-turned towards her father, gazing across at Derek Parker who was mouthing something to her from behind his mother's back.

'Sharon! You're not even listening!'

Several people swung their heads round at the sound of Mrs Holmes' raised voice. Sharon blushed and pulled at her skirt. Miss Keble looked at her watch a little nervously.

Mrs Holmes put on her glasses. 'What you said here, about Sharon being preoccupied with other things. What did you mean, exactly?'

'Well, I've noticed myself and some of the other teachers have said that Sharon has a tendency to switch off in the middle of things. As if there are other things on her mind that she considers to be more important.'

Mrs Holmes grunted. 'She's too worried about boys and

going out. That's her trouble. Jack, we'll have to make sure she stays in until these exams are over, that's all there is to it.'

'Mum!'

Miss Keble began to look a little worried. She shifted her chair to one side. 'I don't know what happens outside school, of course, Mrs Holmes, but Sharon's never struck me as being all that interested in boys at all. Certainly not as much as some of them we've got.'

Mrs Holmes folded her arms emphatically and said nothing. Miss Keble glanced from her watch to the queue forming behind.

'Right, come along, Maureen, Sharon.' Mr Holmes picked up the report and refolded it; he stood up, offered his hand. 'Thank you very much, Miss, er, Keble. We'll have a talk to her. Do what we can. Won't we, Maureen?'

Mrs Holmes pushed her chair back into the table.

'I hope you're feeling better, Mrs Holmes,' said the teacher.

Sharon's mother looked at her surprised. 'Better? Better? There's not been...'

Miss Keble stood up, flustered. 'Oh, I'm sorry, I thought...'

'What've you been saying, Sharon?'

Sharon turned her face away.

'It's my mistake, Mrs Holmes. I must have got confused with somebody else. I'm sorry.' She picked up her biro and put the cap in place. 'I hope I'll see you both again. Cheerio. Goodbye, Sharon.'

Sharon looked at her guiltily, not knowing what to say. Her father took her by the arm and moved her away.

On the journey back, Sharon sat in the back of the car, pushed up into one corner. It was raining; not heavily, just steady, slanting lines of rain. Sharon rubbed her hand against the window and stared out.

Neither her mother nor her father spoke.

*

Her father hadn't even had time to shut the front door when it started. There were going to be changes made; she'd had it all her own way for too long; who did she think she was, ignoring everything her parents and teachers told her?

In future she would do her homework in the kitchen where they could make sure that it was actually getting done. No television until it was all finished and no going out in the week. Fridays and Saturdays she could stay out until eleven, so long as they knew where she was going and who she was going with.

They stood on either side of her; her father still with his jacket on; her mother opening and closing the fingers of her right hand, an unopened packet of cigarettes in the left.

'All right, Sharon?'

She looked from one to the other and back again. She couldn't believe it. What was she expected to say?

She went to walk between them; her father stopped her, his hand on her shoulder.

'Is that all right, Sharon?'

She whirled round, pulling herself away from him.

'All right? All right? Of course it isn't all right! How can it be? I'm goin' to be treated like a prisoner in my own home, aren't I? What's all right about that? How would you like it? S'pose someone come along and said you couldn't go up the pub with your mates or to one of them Tupperware parties or whatever it is you go to. How would you feel? Would you feel all right?'

She was standing with her back to the door, her face was white and her head to one side. Both hands were knotted into the sides of her skirt.

Her parents looked at her wide-eyed, uncomprehending.

Sharon sniffed and wiped at her top lip with the back of one hand. She wasn't going to cry. Not this time she wasn't.

'Sharon, I'd think you'd better go to your room. There's no point in talking about this while you're being perfectly unreasonable.'

'But I'm not being unreasonable. It's you that's . . .'

'How dare you! How dare you!'

'Maureen, don't!'

Mrs Holmes turned on her husband. A fleck of spittle flew from her lips and landed on his sleeve. 'That's it. You take her side. Stick up for her like you always do!'

'I am not taking her side!'

'What else are you doing?'

'I'm trying to get her to see reason.'

'Huh!'

She moved round her husband and grabbed hold of the kettle. He stepped towards Sharon, shaking his head.

'We're doing this for your own good. You might not be able to see that now, but one day you will.'

'I wonder if she'll ever have sufficient gumption to see anything,' put in her mother from the sink.

Mr Holmes went on, ignoring her. 'Those exams. Those G.C.E.s. You can't get anywhere without them. Get your English and maths and I can get you into our place. In the offices.'

The kettle was banged down on to the side.

'I don't want to work in your offices.'

'Any office.'

'I don't want to work in any office.'

'She doesn't know what she wants. You're wasting your time, Jack. You are. She's not worth talking to when she's like this.'

'That's what you say.'

'I've told you before about answering me back, young lady. And what was that your teacher was saying about me being ill? What had you been telling her?'

'Nothing.'

'You must have said something.'

'I didn't.'

'Lying now, along with everything else.'

'Maureen, the woman did say she might have made a mistake.'

'Huh, it's not her that made the mistake!'

'What's that supposed to mean?'

'It doesn't matter.'

Mrs Holmes took the cups and saucers from the shelf and began pouring out the tea. Sharon turned to go.

'Sit down and have your tea.'

'I don't want any tea.'

Sharon went through the door and ran upstairs. Mr Holmes looked up at his wife. 'Let her go, love.'

They heard the bedroom door bang.

'Leave her for a bit.'

Mrs Holmes passed him across his cup of tea and took her own into the living-room.

Half an hour later Mr Holmes put his head round the living-room door. 'I'm off to bed. I'm on early in the morning.'

Mrs Holmes looked at him, saying nothing.

He nodded upwards. 'Should I go in and see how she is, d'you think?'

'Suit yourself. She's your daughter.'

He shut the door behind him and went upstairs; from outside Sharon's room he could hear the sound of her crying. After a few moments he went in.

Sharon was in bed, curled to one side, the sheet covering most of her face. She didn't look round when he closed the door behind him and walked to the bed.

He sat down in the space left by her body. With one hand he lifted the sheet back. Her eyes were red and sore. She looked young; younger than he had seen her for a long time.

'Dad?'

'Um?'

'Nothing.'

He sat there for a while, just looking at her. She was still making little sobbing noises, not really crying, yet not still. He brushed the hair away from her face with his hand. Stood up.

' 'Night, Sharon. Try and get to sleep.'

When her father had gone she moved her hands on to the warm place where he'd been sitting.

She'd wanted him to hold her.

Hold her.

Hold her . . .

5

On the following night Sharon's father was working late. It was also the evening her mother regularly went round to her friend's to have a gossip and look at things in her catalogue.

This Tuesday it seemed as if Mrs Holmes had changed her mind. Half past seven. Eight o'clock. Half past eight. The sound of the television percolated through the wall into the kitchen where Sharon sat in front of a map of the North Downs. Why didn't she go out!

Not that this was the sort of day when anything was going to go right. Miss Keble had been in a bad mood, snapping and shouting at them whenever they came near their form room. At lunchtime, Debbie had been going round flaunting the strip of photos she'd had taken with Mick in the booth in Woolie's : two grinning faces, one above the other. Stupid! And when she'd wanted to talk to Teresa, she'd been off school.

Sharon glanced at the clock on the wall; noticed her mother's handbag lying on top of the cupboard. She picked up her pencil and put a sheet of tracing paper over the map and began drawing a contour line, tongue pushed into one side of her mouth in concentration.

She was on the fourth line when the kitchen door opened suddenly behind her and Sharon's arm jerked upwards, skidding the pencil through the paper and tearing it.

'Shit!'

Her mother's reaction was automatic; Sharon cowered down in her chair, holding the side of her head where she'd been slapped.

'Don't you dare let me hear you using language like that in this house!'

Sharon turned on her, defiant. 'It was your fault.'

'How can it be my fault?'

'Look what you did to my map.'

'I didn't touch your precious map.'

'You made me do it, coming in like that.'

'Oh, I've got to ask permission to come into my own kitchen now, have I?'

'You're the one who shut me in here. Besides, it's my home as much as yours.'

Her mother glared at her, fingers of her right hand opening and closing. 'Oh, it is, is it? Well, you'd better learn how to respect it then, hadn't you? And that means not using that kind of language. Anyone would think you'd been dragged up in the gutter!'

'Yes, they would wouldn't they.'

Sharon's mother raised her hand, swung her arm back. Sharon stood and stared at her, daring her.

'If you don't learn to behave yourself it won't be your home for much longer.'

Mrs Holmes let her arm fall to her side, swung her head and went out of the kitchen with a slam of the door that made the wall shake.

Sharon's hands were pressed to her sides, fingers grinding into her palms. She was breathing irregularly, noisily, rocking very slightly backwards and forwards. After a few minutes she sat down and leaned forward on her arms. She could hear her mother moving around upstairs.

Sharon pushed back her chair: slowly, quietly, she got up.

The bag was dark blue leather. Two large sections with a smaller one in the middle. A metal clasp, the gold paint of which was flaking. Sharon looked at the shut door; listened to the tap running upstairs. She opened the bag.

The centre was the part her mother used as a purse. One pound note, folded over then over again; a fifty p piece; two tens and some ones and twos. She looked in the right-hand side. Tucked down beside a letter and some unused tissues, new, bright, five-pound notes.

Sharon turned towards the door, mouth open, skin dry and burning, her fingers stuck to the money.

After a moment she released her breath slowly. There were five notes : twenty-five pounds. They looked as though they had just been taken from the bank or her mother's post office account. Brand new. Folded just once inside each other. Maybe they were to pay for something she'd ordered from Mrs Jameson's catalogue.

Sharon took two of the notes, replacing the others next to the letter. Shut the bag. Quickly she went back to the table, pushing the ten pounds into the back of her geography book.

She took another sheet of tracing paper from her bag and tried to settle it over the contour lines, aware that her hands were shaking.

Her mother came back downstairs and opened the door. She stood behind Sharon's shoulder, saying, doing nothing. The pencil wavered as Sharon held her breath, sure that somehow her mother knew, that she had seen. Instead Mrs Holmes walked round the table and stopped by the cup-board.

'Sharon?'

'Mm?'

'Don't sit up doing that for too long. I want you in bed by ten.'

Sharon tried to keep her eyes on the map; tried not to look at the bag.

'Did you hear that?'

'Yes.'

Mrs Holmes picked up her bag and went out. Sharon sat there listening to the echo of the front door being pulled to, footsteps down the path. She opened the book and looked at the notes. At the clock.

She hurried upstairs.

*

By the time Sharon got to the station it was drizzling. She squinted her eyes as she climbed the steps alongside the dull orange walls of the leisure centre. Cars swished under the bridge in both directions. Sharon transferred her bag from one hand to the other. She hadn't taken very much, yet the case was already feeling heavy. She had walked down to the station, not wanting to risk meeting anyone she knew on the bus.

Past the shuttered kiosk and up to the window of the ticket office.

'London, please.'

She put one of the five pound notes down and the man spun the metal plate. Sharon picked up her ticket; put her change in her purse.

The youth at the barrier had strands of dark, greasy hair falling down towards his shoulders from under a uniform cap. He winked at Sharon and punched a round hole in her ticket.

'Through train in about twenty minutes. Number three.'

The waiting-room was steamed over, moisture running down the glass from the inside. The blurred shapes of people, luggage; a baby crying. Sharon walked back past the steps. Despite the rain, a man was sitting on a bench out in the open, his coat collar pulled up, a dark duffle bag on the seat beside him.

Sharon stood under the stairs, her bag resting on a low trolley. What if her mother came back early? What would she do? Probably wait till her father got back from work – by which time Sharon would be in London. Safe at her nan's. In Walthamstow. She would go there. Explain why she'd done it. Why she'd run away.

Run away.

The two words went round inside Sharon's head. One of the girls in the fifth year had run away. Diane Cherry. She'd collected her wages from her Saturday job in the shoe shop and hitched a lift up the motorway. All on account of some boy she'd met in the summer. He was working on a fair that came and set up on the open ground near their school. Collecting money on the dodgems, jumping over the fronts of cars as they swung round, standing on the bumpers, one hand on the pole.

Sharon remembered him. Long, greasy hair – black and thick, falling past the collar of his old leather waistcoat. Nothing underneath that : only a dark chest matted with hair and a tattoo over his heart. A chain and anchor with his name curling round it in swirly lettering. Deep blue, it was. Eddie.

She'd been with Debbie and Heather. They'd been getting on all right with her then. Heather had been calling out to him, real saucy. Asking for it, really.

But he'd gone off with Diane instead. She'd been there with this bloke from the tech that she'd been going out with for nearly three months. Just told him she was chucking him. Right then.

When the fair shut down that night, Diane went off with this Eddie somewhere. Into the woods across from the fairground, probably. Didn't get home till gone two.

Sharon had heard Diane telling her mates about it in the loo the first day back at school. How he was better than anybody else she'd ever been with and he was going to come back for her when the fair shut down for the end of the summer.

The other girls all said 'Really?' and 'Go on' and 'Great!', but none of them believed it. That he'd bother with her again. Next thing, she'd gone. Apparently, he'd sent her a letter and asked her to come up to Doncaster, which was where the fair was.

Her parents only found out about the letter afterwards.

They'd had the police searching for her and everything. This bloke remembered giving her a lift up the motorway to Newark or somewhere like that.

Anyway, Diane's dad went up there to see her, fetch her home. She was in this caravan; she'd been living there with

Eddie ever since she'd run off. She just looked at her dad and said she wasn't coming.

There was this great row and Eddie came bursting in in the middle of it. He had a go at Diane's dad and cut the side of his head open. After that the police were called and there was all kinds of trouble.

They were all for charging Eddie with assault and rape and everything. In the end Diane's dad said he wouldn't press charges if she came back home with him. Her being under age and all made it difficult. She agreed to go back.

After a week at home, she got transferred to another school. She said she was going to run away again. Meet up with Eddie down in Cornwall somewhere.

Probably she would.

Sharon listened : there was a train coming. She stuck her head out into the rain. The lights shone dully, getting closer. People started to come out of the waiting-room. The announcement came over the loudspeaker. Sharon picked up her case and walked down to the end of the platform, past the man on the bench, who still hadn't moved.

She got into the front carriage. There were tables between the seats; the inside looked new. In the corner a couple were sitting with their heads leaning against one another. The girl was sleeping, her mouth open slightly; the man opened his eyes and looked out without shifting the position of his head.

Half way along on the left a middle-aged woman sat doing a crossword. There wasn't anybody else in the carriage. Sharon went and sat opposite the woman, one seat further forward. As the train moved out she opened her case and took out a copy of *Jackie*.

Five minutes later a ticket collector came along and asked her for her ticket. He looked at it and put it into his pocket.

Sharon's stomach turned in a quick moment of panic.

'What about getting off?'

He smiled. He was a short West Indian with a round face and bright eyes.

'Walk right through at King's Cross. Okay?'

Sharon nodded, and he walked back down the train, whistling.

Sooner than she had thought, they were pulling into London. She folded her magazine and put it back in her case. The couple in the corner were both awake now, holding hands and standing by the door. The woman looked up at Sharon suddenly. Her eyes moved over Sharon's face, clothes, the case on the table. Expressionless.

Sharon picked up the case by the handle and hurried past her to stand by the couple who were now out between the carriages, window down, ready to get off.

There had been more people further back on the train than she'd imagined. For a few moments she was lost in a moving huddle of passengers, heavy suitcases and pushchairs. Someone banged something into the back of her leg and shouted, 'Sorry.' Almost before she'd realized, Sharon was through the barrier and standing in the entrance hall. She looked up at the clock over the train departures board. Not far off eleven o'clock. By the time she got to her nan's it would be really late.

Her nan lived by herself and she was sure to be in bed. Maybe she wouldn't come to the door and let her in. No, of course she would : that was silly.

Sharon had already worked out that she'd go on the underground, though whenever she'd visited her nan before it had always been with her parents and they'd gone in the car. Usually, though, it was the other way round. They would go and meet her nan at the station; struggling up the steps with at least three bags in her hands, stopping to catch her breath, wearing the dark blue hat with a little feather – the one she kept for best.

One of the bags would always have some present for Sharon tucked away and as soon as she got the chance, her nan would kiss her and say, 'Hello, love, it's nice to see you.'

Whenever she kissed Sharon, her breath always had a slightly sickly smell to it.

Sharon saw the sign for the underground. She was most of the way down the stairs, when she started at the sound of running feet and shouting. A gang of youths rushed round the corner, boots clipping on the hard floor. They headed for the stairs and Sharon stood where she was, petrified.

The first two or three ducked round her, mouths open, red, yelling. The next one thumped into her shoulder, sending her sideways against the wall.

'Let's get 'er!'

'Yea, give 'er one.'

'Leave it out! Wouldn't touch 'er with yours!'

Half a dozen of them stood in front of her, circling her, blocking her in. A man wearing a dark suit and carrying a brief-case hurried past on the opposite side, head averted.

One of the youths stuck two fingers up at his back. 'Poof!'

'Bender!'

'Wanker! Wanker! Wanker!'

Sharon tried to push her way between two of them, using her case.

''Ere, she don't reckon us.'

'Don't you reckon us, darlin'?'

They had blue and white soccer scarves tied to their belts and hanging down by their legs. One was wearing a large cap in blue and white sections.

'That's all right, 'cause we don't reckon you. Scabby cow!'

A hand pushed at her arm and Sharon went back hard against the wall, dropping her case.

''Ere, look what we've got.'

'Bung it, Tel.'

'Over 'ere! Over 'ere!'

They spread out, hurling the case up and down the steps. One of them dropped it and kicked it across the floor, into the tiled wall. Sharon didn't dare move away from the wall, arms pressed back against it, hands open.

The youths who had rushed past into the main line station reappeared.

'Over the other side. Come on. Quick!'

They tore away round the curve of the subway and out of sight. Sharon's small case lay close to the foot of the steps, one corner dented in. As she picked it up there was a loud shouting from ahead of her; she turned and hurried back up to the entrance of the main station.

Sharon moved quickly away from the top of the stairs, weaving between the wooden seats. A drunk lurched up in front of her, pawing the air. She ducked to the right, banging her leg against a pile of cases. The man fell backwards, as though in slow motion; his head hit the floor and didn't move again. No one went to help him, even looked interested.

Sharon saw a policewoman standing on the other side of a pair of glass double doors.

Maybe there was some other way of getting down to the underground.

She walked quickly past the tea bar at the corner and turned along by a blackened wall and past a line of trolleys piled high with bundles of newspapers.

She was out in the street. Further up the road on the left there was a pub with its lights still on. Two cars parked close to one another, empty.

Traffic on the main road to the right; the sound of some-one singing. 'They shoot horses, don't they?' The same line, over and over and over.

Sharon leaned against the wall, closed her eyes. She didn't want to be here. She didn't want to be at home. She had thought she wanted to be at her nan's but that was miles away and it was getting later all the time.

She didn't know where to go – what to do.

The wall had made the sleeve of her coat dirty. She wet her fingers and rubbed at the mark, smudging it. She could feel the tears readying themselves behind her eyes.

Heard a sound behind her.

Turned.

An old woman with grey hair stood between the trolleys and the far wall. She was wearing a torn old coat and holding a bottle in one hand. She said something that Sharon didn't understand and held the bottle out towards her, smiling.

Sharon was about to turn away and go back towards the street when she thought how stupid she was being. What if Mick Tracey could see her now? Or Teresa?

Sharon tightened her grip on the case and walked past the old woman, who was still smiling and offering her bottle, and into the station concourse. There were lots of people milling about; a train must have just come in, an express, inter-city.

Sharon found an unoccupied seat, under the lights of the departures board, and sat at the end of it, her case on the floor beside her. Someone walked past close and she picked the case up and put it on her lap. She realized that she was feeling really tired, nervy. Sharon hugged the case to herself and tried to think.

'Are you all right, miss?'

Sharon jumped. The policewoman stood beside her, peaked cap, uniform pressed and smart. Fair hair showing under the cap; mouth set in a tight line. She didn't seem to have any lips at all.

Sharon looked up, nodded.

'Sure, are you?'

'Mmm.'

She held the case even more tightly until she saw that the woman was staring at her hands.

'By yourself?'

'Yes. But . . . but I'm just going home.'

'Where's home?'

'Stevenage.' The word came out before she had the chance to think.

'By yourself, are you?'

'Yes.' She looked at the woman's inquiring eyes; knew that

she wasn't satisfied. 'I've been to see me nan. She lives in Walthamstow.'

'Got a ticket, then?'

'Yes. No.'

'No?'

Sharon shook her head.

'You might as well get one now, then, hadn't you?' She turned her head and read along the board. 'Your train goes in ten minutes.'

Go away, thought Sharon, go away!

But she knew that the woman wouldn't.

Sharon stood up slowly and looked around for the ticket office. The policewoman pointed to the sign, then followed her over. Stood close enough to hear what she said to the clerk and watch her pay.

'It's on the other platforms,' the woman said. 'The suburban ones through there.'

Again she pointed.

'Someone meeting you, are they?' she called when Sharon was five or so yards away.

'Yea. Yes. Me dad.'

Sharon hustled over the cobbles and into the dingy part of the station where the stopping trains went from. Hers was already in. An Indian with a small, dark face stopped talking to two friends and clipped her ticket.

There were already quite a lot of people on the train; the lights were only dimly on. Sharon chose the middle of three carriages and sat in a double seat next to the window. It was the only one unoccupied.

She put her case alongside her and pressed her clenched hands down between her knees, desperate to stop shaking.

6

The train was slow, too hot and filling with smoke. Sharon sat there counting off the stations to herself, trying not to think about what had happened, what would happen when she got home.

Home.

She wasn't going. Couldn't. Not now. In the middle of the night, bedraggled on the doorstep, case in hand. She could see her mother's face, hear her father's bewildered anger. It would be like before, only worse.

No.

After Hatfield she fell asleep: suddenly: totally. When the movement of the train jolted her awake Sharon thought she'd been sleeping for hours. They were pulling out of a station and she rubbed at the steamed-over window, staring frantically out, trying to read the name.

Welwyn North.

Next stop then.

Her mind started racing, taking her in circles she was unable to stop or understand. The skin on the backs of her hands and at the roots of her hair seemed to burn; she was covered by a dry sweat. She rubbed at the back of her neck, her left eye. Her mouth opened, finding it difficult to breathe.

For one moment Sharon thought that she'd cried out, but no one else in the carriage had moved, turned round. It had been inside her own head.

The train began to slow down. Sharon stood up, glanced hastily at the others preparing to get off. She didn't know them.

On the platform she hurried forward, head down, not looking to left or right. She was the first up the stairs and through the gap by the ticket collector's cubicle.

Ten yards on she halted. Below, to the left, the shapes of people queuing for a taxi. Ahead, the bridge, the rain, and beyond that, the town.

If only ... if only ...

Sharon stared at the light that showed through the curtains of the downstairs window. All of the other houses were dark, silent. She had no idea what time it was, nor how long she had been standing where she was.

She shifted her weight from one foot to the other; every so often they would ache, threaten to go numb. The muscles at the backs of her calves ached too. The light was still on.

She imagined her parents inside, sitting on either side of the kitchen table. Drinking tea. Her mother smoking in short, nervy puffs, hardly inhaling at all.

Don't you let me catch you smoking, young lady!

The first time Sharon had been ten. One of her mates at the juniors had stolen some from a packet she'd found in her dad's raincoat. After school they'd wandered up to the park and gone past the thicker bushes at the far side of the adventure playground.

They'd lit one and passed it round.

Sharon had inhaled by mistake; she'd folded in half, coughing and reaching until she was sure she'd be sick. She hadn't been. One of the others had, though. They'd had to tell the teacher, the girl had been so bad. They'd said nothing about the cigarette; claimed it was school dinners.

It hadn't been till the summer holiday before going to secondary school that she'd smoked a whole cigarette on her own. When she and her parents got back from holiday in Devon, her mum had suddenly started smoking. Sharon had been amazed.

Don't let me catch you smoking, young lady!

Once she overheard an argument between her parents

about it. Her mum had said it was her nerves; said it was no wonder, seeing what she had to put up with.

Sharon had taken one of her mother's and smoked it lying in the long grass close by the water tower. She hadn't liked it much. After that she'd hardly bothered. A few times when the others did and she hadn't wanted to feel left out.

A telephone was ringing. Sharon was uncertain how long it had been going on for. She guessed that it was coming from her house. It stopped. Had they got fed up with waiting or had one of her parents answered it?

It could be the police. They would have told the police by now, she was certain.

She thought again about Diane Cherry. At least she'd gone somewhere, done something. Diane hadn't been a silly coward; she hadn't run back again.

Back again and done what? Wandered around for an hour or more, then walked home and stood up the road, frightened to go and ring the bell, knock on the door. Not even wanting to, but without an idea of what else to do either.

Diane and her Eddie.

Was that what she wanted?

Sharon tried to imagine going off with Mick Tracey. Living with him in a caravan in Darlington or Doncaster or wherever it had been. She shuddered, but it might have been the cold.

Sharon jammed her eyes shut.

When she reopened them the kitchen light had been switched off: Two, three seconds, then the bedroom light went on. She saw her father clearly as he drew the curtains. She was unable to move back around the corner. He finished closing the curains : he hadn't noticed her.

The light stayed on. Sharon wondered if they were talking, talking about her, or whether they were lying there in silence. Lying side by side : not touching. She could not remember, at that moment, seeing her parents touch each other.

The lights went out. The house a house like all the others.

Sharon walked down past it and headed back towards the town centre.

Really tired now, moving slowly from one shop window to another. Concentrating on the things on display. Don't think much of that. That'd be all right. Curry's. Chelsea Girl. Dorothy Perkins'. Smith's.

Sharon turned away from the wide frontage of Boot's and looked at the fountain. Lights and water off. Deserted. Spreading out around her, unseen, thousands of houses. People asleep. Families.

The two policemen were standing outside the Co-op, one of them checking the doors, the other facing outwards, staring directly at Sharon. For a second she thought of running, but knew it would do no good.

One policeman tapped the other, said something Sharon couldn't hear. Because there seemed nothing else to do, she walked slowly over towards them.

She'd been surprised at how they'd treated her at the police station. The two who'd taken her there in their car had treated it all as a big joke. Teased her and laughed. But they hadn't been annoyed, or unkind really. Inside the new police station, across from the leisure centre, it was much busier than she'd imagined for that time of the morning. Someone had brought her a cup of tea and then this young police-woman had come and talked to her. Asked questions, making notes on a spiral pad, using a pencil.

Sharon told her everything that had happened : almost everything. Talking about it only reminded her, made it real. More real. She spoke quietly, hesitating every now and then when the woman asked her for reasons.

Why had she decided to run off that night in particular?

Why had she caught the train back?

Trying to explain herself, Sharon was aware that her answers sounded flat, thin, unimportant. Yet she knew that was not so. They were important.

The policewoman wrote it all down, smiled once or twice. Sounded sympathetic.

'Like another cup of tea?' she asked when it was over.

'No, thanks.'

'Come on, then.'

Sharon looked across the table, blinked apprehensively. The policewoman stood up and smoothed down her uniform with both hands.

'Where?'

'We'd better get you home.'

Sharon looked round the room, down to the note pad, back to the woman's face. 'Do they . . . ?'

She nodded. 'We phoned them. They're expecting you.'

The woman put an arm round Sharon as they got to the door, gave her a quick squeeze. 'Cheer up, love.'

Her father was standing on the path that led from the front door. Trousers, carpet slippers, cardigan over his pyjama jacket. In the comparative darkness his face looked exceptionally white. When Sharon got nearer, she could see her mother in the doorway. She had her blue dressing gown on, the one she'd bought specially for going into the hospital that time. Her eyes were red.

Sharon stopped and the policewoman gave her a gentle push.

Standing alongside her father, looking not at him but at the stubs of rose bushes he had put in the front garden that weekend, she managed, 'Dad, I'm . . . I'm . . .'

Then the tears took her. She walked on towards the figure of her mother. She reached out for the side of the door, a hand took the suitcase away from her and then she was in the living-room, sitting in her father's chair, letting it all drain wordlessly out of her.

Someone came in and switched the fire on; set a cup of tea on the table in front of her. In the kitchen her parents were talking to the policewoman. Sharon didn't know what they were saying; did not care.

70

Her hands pulled at an arm of the chair, hugging it into her side until she could feel it hard against her ribs. Till it hurt. Her head rocked back and forwards, turned from side to side. She cried in great gulping sobs, gasping for air, eyes opening and closing.

No.

No!

'No!'

The door was pushed open and her father came in quickly, staring at her.

Sharon turned her face up towards him : through the blur of tears all she could see clearly was his anger.

'Is she all right?' The policewoman's voice from the hall.

'Yes.' The word fell like a stone.

A few moments later the front door opened and closed. Sharon knew her father was still standing above her, close to the chair, but she kept her head averted.

Her mother came into the room and shut the door; went over to her own chair and sat down.

She heard her father sigh and go across to the settee. 'You didn't drink your tea, Sharon. It'll be . . .'

'Never mind about the tea. What we want is an explanation.'

'Maureen, don't you think we should . . .'

'What?'

'Wait?'

Her mother laughed, almost a snort. 'Wait! That's good. What do you think we've been doing, up all night? Worrying ourselves sick.'

You haven't been up all night, Sharon thought, you went to bed.

She didn't say anything. She still had one hand firmly on the arm of the chair; the other was rubbing at her face, her eyes. She avoided looking at either of them.

'An explanation,' her mother repeated.

Silence, then : 'Well, Sharon, what did you do it for?'

She hung her head. Anything she said would be no good. Either they'd shout back at her, tell her it was nonsense, stupid – or they'd ask more questions and then more still. Why? Why?

She glanced at her father and then away, down at the cold cup of tea, untouched.

'You must have had a reason?'

Her mother lit a cigarette and blew the smoke up towards the ceiling.

'Where did you think you were going to go in London?'

'Me nan's.' She hadn't meant to tell them.

'What on earth were you going there for?'

'Worrying her. What was she supposed to do with you? Apart from send you packing back to us.'

'I don't understand you, Sharon, I honestly don't. I should have thought you'd have more sense.'

Mrs Holmes stubbed out her cigarette in the ashtray. 'Then there's the matter of the money.'

Sharon thought her father was going to say something, but he didn't.

She wiped the back of her hand across her face, sniffing; looked at her mother.

'You stole it, didn't you?'

Sharon pursed her lips together.

'You needn't bother denying it. You took it from my purse before I went out. There I was opening my bag to pay Mrs Jameson and there was ten pounds missing. I didn't know where to put myself. I felt a proper fool.'

'Maureen, that's not the point. Not for now.'

'Of course it's the point!' Mrs Holmes leaned forward, pointing at Sharon. 'She stole money from my bag and went gallivanting up to London with it for God alone knows what reason.'

She stood up. 'Who were you meeting, Sharon?'

'I wasn't meeting anyone. I told you ...'

'She's told us ...'

'Going to her nan's! Do you expect me to believe that? What on earth would she want to go there for?' She pushed the table out of the way with her leg and stood right in front of Sharon, leaning down. 'You were going to meet someone, weren't you? Weren't you?'

'No!'

Mrs Holmes slapped at her face, missing and striking the top of her shoulder and the side of her neck.

'Don't you scream at me. You were meeting some boy and he didn't turn up.'

'Maureen, you've no proof of that. Why couldn't she have been doing what she said?'

'If she was going to her nan's why didn't she go? Why did she come back and spend the night wandering around the town? Getting into God knows what trouble.'

'I haven't been in any trouble.'

Mrs Holmes turned round, kicking against the table, hands up to her face. She stood against the far wall, crying.

'See,' her father said. 'See what you've done to your mother.'

7

The plimsoll slammed into the partition wall at the side of the classroom.

'Who slung that?'

Derek Parker sat round sideways at his desk in the front corner, staring back across the room. The plimsoll lay on its side behind him.

At the opposite corner, Kevin and Earl were gazing down at a copy of *Fury* much too intently. Derek reached down for the plimsoll and balanced it in his right hand for a few seconds.

'Kev!'

The shoe landed on the desk between their heads, ripping a page of the comic out of the staples and bouncing hard against Earl's chest.

'What d'you do that for, you stupid sod?'

'You shouldn't 'ave chucked it at me, should you?'

'Who chucked it at you?'

'You did! One of you.'

'Piss off!'

'Don't you tell me to piss off, you black bastard!'

Earl snatched at the plimsoll and hurled it back, wildly. It went high across the middle of the room and smashed against the painting on the wall. The heel had gouged out a sharp section of sky, a slice of sea.

'Now look what...'

The door opened: Miss Keble stood there, register under one arm, the other folded in front of herself, balancing a pile of exercise books. Earl and Derek Parker were standing, anger showing on their faces; Kevin had ducked down behind his desk, lid up.

The form teacher stood there, taking it all in.

She walked slowly to the front of the room and put her things down on her wide desk. Glanced back up at the painting.

'It's typical, isn't it?'

Faces looked at other faces, at tops of desks, at the floor, at something suddenly interesting inside their bags.

'Typical.'

Sharon shuffled her feet and accidentally knocked her bag over.

'And for heaven's sake, sit still!' Miss Keble stared at Sharon, her hands spread wide on the top of her desk. Sharon, feeling herself beginning to go red, looked away.

'All it needs is for me to be a few minutes late coming in for registration and you're doing your well-known impersonation of a roomful of five-year-olds.'

The teacher picked up the plimsoll.

'Yours, Derek? Or Earl, yours perhaps?'

'No, Miss.'

'Not mine.'

'Of course not. How silly of me to have thought it would be. Or that you would own up to it, if it were.'

Earl stood with hands behind his back, looking out of the window on the far side. Derek Parker looked back at Miss Keble sullenly.

'Sit down. Sit down, the pair of you.'

Sharon quietly righted her bag, feeling down to the bottom to make sure that nothing had rolled out.

'The two of you can come and see me at break.'

She raised a hand and quelled the moans of complaint.

'We'll see what we can do about arranging for you to get along to Mr Williams and explain to him how you came to ruin one of the paintings he'd lent us. Doubtless he and I will be able to think of some suitable means of making up for what happened. Like cleaning out the art rooms for a week.'

'Go on, Miss!'

'That's not fair.'

Miss Keble hit the underside of the plimsoll down onto the desk and Sharon jumped.

'Not fair! What do you mean, not fair? That's the trouble with you, isn't it. All of you.' She swept a dismissive look round the room. 'You think you can go ahead and do what you like and ignore the consequences. Just hang your head and mumble something you don't mean about being sorry and everything will be all right. Well, it's time you learnt that it won't.'

She stood straighter, pressing back her shoulder blades.

Someone coughed : Earl and Kevin nudged each other. Debbie and Heather were trying not to look at one another, both of them on the verge of bursting into laughter.

'You go moaning on about being treated like children, about how you ought to be treated like adults – and this is what you do. How you behave. It's about time you decided to grow up. If you stopped behaving like kids, you might stand a chance of not being treated like them.'

Miss Keble sat down and called out the names on the register. When Debbie Bradley did begin to giggle, one shout of her name was enough to shut her up again. Sharon sat twisting her fingers, pressing the backs of her wrists down into her lap, bag between her legs.

'All right. Off into assembly. Quickly now.'

The class stood up, muted. Moved towards the door resentfully, casting glances at the three boys who had got them into trouble. Beginning to mutter as they got into the corridor and merged with other forms.

Sharon hesitated between her desk and Miss Keble's. The teacher was totalling the figures at the bottom of the register.

'Well, Sharon?'

'Nothing, Miss.'

'Hurry up, then. You'll be late.'

Sharon left the classroom and headed for the hall. At the

end of the corridor, she turned left and went into the girls'
toilet.

Sharon sat with her eyes closed. The outer door banged
open and a tap went on, water splashing. Off again. Sound
of the door being slammed shut.

Sharon opened her eyes and reached down into her bag.
The bottle had been new a week ago; now it looked about
three quarters full. She held it in the flat of her right hand,
reading the label, not seeing, understanding a word.

Assembly would go on for ten minutes, possibly more.

The bottle was transferred to the other hand; Sharon un-
screwed the white metal top and dropped it back down into
the bag. Her breathing had quickened; she pulled at the
front of her hair, then put the bottle back in her right hand.

Someone walked past heavily. The teacher on duty.

Come on. Come on!

The first three aspirins lay in her left hand. The vein at the
right side of her head was throbbing and she put the bottle
against it. Cool. Smooth.

Sharon opened her mouth and put her left hand up to it.
Her lips closed round the tablets, taking them in. There was
no saliva; the back of her throat felt dry.

She crunched down against the aspirin with her teeth. It
tasted bitter and immediately she wanted to spit it out. The
bottle was still against the side of her head. She swallowed
the pieces down, poking her tongue around the back of her
teeth, the gaps between teeth and gums.

She tipped another four into the middle of her hand.
Closed her eyes. Pushed them into her mouth. Bit down.
Chewed. Swallowed.

It was going to take ages like this.

Next time she put the bottle straight to her mouth, took in
more. Stopped. For some reason it seemed important that she
knew how many. With the tip of her finger she counted the
tablets on her tongue. Five.

Twelve altogether then.

Sharon went back to putting them in her hand first : sixteen, twenty, twenty-five, twenty-eight.

In a sudden panic Sharon thought she'd been sitting there too long. They'd come streaming in at any minute, on their way back from assembly. Laughing and swopping stories about what they'd got up to the night before.

She thought about Debbie; Debbie and Mick. Mick and herself. Mick kissing her, pushing his tongue between her teeth, like her own which now edged the fragments of aspirin back into her mouth. Mick getting hold of her breasts so that it hurt. Grabbing at her legs.

Tight cow!

Sharon reached out and steadied herself against the toilet wall.

Forty-seven. Fifty-four.

Her dad ...

Sixty.

Low down on the wall, on the right hand side, someone had drawn a man's penis in biro. Sharon wondered why she hadn't noticed it before.

Sixty-five.

For a moment her body jerked forward and she imagined that she was going to be sick. The bottle fell from her fingers and she gripped both sides of the toilet seat hard. Rocked backwards, forwards. Steadied herself, mouth open drawing in air.

She picked up the bottle. One, no, two of the tablets had come out and rolled towards the door. She bent forwards and got hold of them.

Sixty-six. Sixty-seven.

The bottle tipped over her palm : empty.

Sharon stared at the last tablets : crunched them between the double teeth at the back of her mouth.

Seventy-two.

She pushed herself up, letting the bottle fall into her

open bag. Turning, she pulled the chain, flushed the toilet.

In the corridor she could hear the hymn at the end of assembly. First lesson was needlework. She walked along the corridor, towards the stairs. Leaning against the bannister, Sharon thought that she might be feeling shaky.

No, she couldn't be, not yet.

Sharon and Teresa were sitting at the same table. Teresa was making a skirt; she'd been working on it for weeks, taking her time. She couldn't afford to throw the money away, she said. She was going to have to wear it so it had better look all right.

Sharon was sewing pockets onto an apron, doing cross-stitching on the edges. She couldn't really see what she was doing; kept stopping, making mistakes.

'You look in a right mood,' said Teresa. 'What's the matter with you?'

Sharon looked at her, head swaying a little.

''Ere, are you all right?'

'Yes. I . . . I don't . . .'

Her arm banged on to the table top; her mouth was slightly open. She was trying to focus on Teresa, finding it difficult.

'You gonna be sick, or somethin'?'

Sharon shook her head slowly.

Teresa pushed her chair closer. 'What's goin' on? What . . . you've done somethin', 'aven't you?' She caught hold of Teresa's arm. 'What've you done. What've you taken? Eh?'

Sharon blinked several times.

Teresa shook her, half standing now. 'Tell me, for Christ's sake! What was it? Paracetemol?'

Sharon shook her head from side to side.

'Aspirin?'

'Yes.'

'How long ago?'

'Assembly.'

Teresa pulled Sharon to her feet. 'How many?'

The words were slow and slurred: but exact. 'Seventy-two.'

Teresa half led her, half pushed her across the room.

'Teresa. Sharon. Where do you think you're going?'

'I'm taking her downstairs. She's sick.'

'But you can't . . .'

The needlework teacher's protest went unheard. Teresa hurried Sharon down the two flights of stairs and along the corridor to the sick room. There was nobody there.

'Sit down. And don't move.'

Teresa ran to the office, nearly knocking two first years over as she rounded the corner.

There were four office staff sitting down, three teachers standing around them, talking.

'Sharon Holmes's taken an overdose. She's in the sick room.'

Silence. Then they began asking her questions, two of them at the same time. Someone went out to check on Sharon. After a few moments, the secretary picked up the phone and dialled the hospital for an ambulance.

'All right, Teresa. Back to your lesson.'

'Can't I wait with Sharon till the ambulance comes?'

'That won't be necessary.'

Teresa turned on her heels and went out, leaving the office door open. She went to the sick room.

'How is she?'

'She'll be all right, I expect.'

Teresa sat down next to Sharon.

'Shouldn't you be back in class?'

'It doesn't matter.'

Sharon had heard Teresa's voice and knew that she was sitting close to her. Someone else as well. The wall opposite kept coming closer and then moving away again. Her hair was falling across her face. She tried to brush it away but kept missing. Someone's hand did it for her.

The next second everything snapped back into focus. Mrs Nicolson. Teresa. She could see both of them clearly. The matt white of the wall. The fingers of her hand pressing against her knee, the hem of her skirt.

'The ambulance'll be here soon,' Teresa said.

'They'll have sent for your mother,' said Mrs Nicolson.

There were two ambulance men and they insisted on putting Sharon on a stretcher, although she said she could walk.

'Not likely,' said the bigger of the pair, 'not worth the risk. Don't want you falling 'ead over 'eels, do we?'

His grin blurred as Sharon looked at him.

'Come on, darlin'. Let's be having you.'

They laid a grey blanket across her and carried her out into the corridor. Sharon felt a hand on her shoulder, but she didn't know whose it was.

There was a lot of talking; there seemed to be people standing on either side of the corridor. Her concentration came and went, things moved in and out of focus.

She wanted to ask Teresa to look after her bag, but she couldn't see her.

'Mind yer backs there, please. Move right down the bus!'

The ambulance man laughed at his own joke.

Sharon turned her head to one side and saw Mick Tracey standing by the entrance to the office, together with two other sixth formers. She could see his face clearly, staring down at her.

'Silly bitch!' he said.

8

'What's the name?'

'Sharon Holmes.'

'Is that the full name?'

'Irene.'

'Sharon Irene Holmes?'

'Yes. Yes, that's right.'

'And the address?'

Questions and answers moved through the space above Sharon's head. She knew it was her mother's voice; her mother strangely unsure, uncertain.

'All right, take off your jewellery.'

The nurse repeated the order. Sharon realized that she meant her. Her jewellery. She tried to sit up.

'Just take it steady now.' Hands helped her. 'That's it, both those rings. Now the necklace – that's pretty, isn't it. We'll have to take those things from your ears. The sleepers, yes. There's a good girl. You'll look after those, Mrs Holmes, will you? Take them home for now.'

Sharon could suddenly see her mum; standing at the end of the bed, whatever it was she was lying on. Didn't seem like a proper bed, really. Drawn, her face was. Sharon blinked, tried to see more clearly. Everything was hazy now. No more fading and clearing. Like a mist all the time. Not thick, though. Not thick.

'Let's get you undressed, then.'

Her mother and the nurse helped her out of her clothes. Taking her tights off she nearly fell and someone caught her.

'Steady, now.'

Sharon lay back on the bed. It felt cold against her skin,

tacky, like plastic. There was a light above the bed: sun through mist.

'Let's get you into this.'

The nurse got hold of her arms, first the right, then the left.

'Lift up a bit, love. That's better. Fine.'

Fingers doing something behind her, pulling things.

'Right, now, Sharon. Listen carefully. Can you hear what I'm saying?'

Sharon nodded; her head felt thick, stuffed with old clothes.

'Your mother's going to take your things away and we'll get all that stuff out of your stomach. She'll be here later. There's nothing to worry about. Okay?'

Sharon nodded once more. Her mother and the nurse said something but she couldn't make out what it was. She looked down at herself. She was wearing a white sort of robe with long sleeves and no buttons or anything. Sharon felt round behind. It was done up at the back; lots of bows.

The nurse bent down in front of her. That was better, less hazy. She looked nice. She looked ...

'Now tell me again, love, how many of those pills did you swallow?'

'Seventy-two.'

'And did you take them down whole with water or did you chew them?'

Sharon closed her eyes. The nurse shook her by the shoulder; not hard.

'Sharon?'

'Yes?'

'How did you ...'

'Chewed them.'

There was another nurse there now; the one who had been talking to her stood up. Sharon pulled at the sleeve of the robe. There was a loose cotton: on the third attempt she caught hold of it.

'What size tube?'

'Over seventy, she says.'

'The largest, then?'

'I think so.'

Sharon let go of the end of cotton. Tube. What tube? What were they going to do? Where were they going to put it? She didn't want a tube.

'Nurse. Nurse. I don't want no tube.'

'Bit late for that. Should have thought of that sooner. Before you did it.' The new voice was sharper.

'Is Gordon there?'

'I saw him a minute ago.'

'Better get him to come and hold her.'

Sharon's throat tightened. She closed her eyes. Wanted to go to sleep. More than anything that was what she wanted.

But she could not go to sleep.

'Move on to your side now, will you, there's a good girl.' Sharon started – a man's voice, quite young though, friendly.

'That's the way. Take a look over your shoulder. Can you see that bar? D'you think you can reach both hands round and catch hold of that for us?'

The metal rail ran along the length of the bed, perhaps six inches above the mattress. It was round and cold, polished chrome. Sharon was lying on her right arm, her hands close together on the bar, the left slightly overlapping the right.

She could see the male nurse now; dressed like a dentist. Brown hair. He smiled at her as he stood there, behind her.

'All right, Gordon?'

He nodded.

'Right,' the nurse went on, 'let's have your head round this way, then.'

Sharon turned and saw the tube.

Immediately she started to pull her hands away from the bar; they were caught fast. A strong grip around the wrists, thumbs pressing into the backs of her hands.

'Take it steady now.'

Sharon closed her eyes tight, wriggled back across the bed.

'We haven't got all day,' she heard one of the nurses say.

'Nor's she.'

'Come on.' said the man. 'Be a good girl. Don't make it any worse. You have to do it, you know.'

Sharon looked at the tube in the nurses's hands. It seemed to be made of some kind of plastic; you could almost see through it. As wide as the end of her finger. Long. Very long. What was ...?

The nurse bent forwards, holding the end of the tube towards Sharon's face.

'Open.'

Sharon shook her head, blinked. Her eyes showed she still didn't understand; did not want to understand.

'Open your mouth.'

The end was under her nose : it smelt of something she knew but could not remember. It touched her lips. Lay against them. With her eyes shut she could feel the shape of it.

The male nurse moved her further across the bed, so that she was almost to the other side, her arms stretched straighter to keep her hands on the rail. His own hands over hers.

'Now all you have to do is to take it into your mouth and swallow. Just keep swallowing until it's gone right down into your stomach.'

Eyes wide, head shaking, Sharon opened her mouth. The tube was between her lips.

A hand on her back, the small of her back.

'Swallow, there's a good girl. Swallow.'

Sharon could feel the tube at the back of her throat. It would never go past there; she knew it wouldn't. Impossible. Impossible. She stretched her mouth wide, the muscles at the rear of the throat; it was like wanting to be sick, like reaching. She made a gurgling, choked sound and the tube was in her neck.

Sounds coming through her nose. Eyes watering. The nurse leaning over her, holding the tube over her head, feeding it down through her opened mouth into her body.

The warm hand over her own.

Sharon looked at the nurse and she could see her clearly. Dark hairs just beyond the corners of her upper lip. A brown mole on her right cheek. No. No, left cheek. The other way round. Hair pinned behind a cap. White cap. She didn't look very old. Not a great deal older than Sharon herself.

Sharon knew that the tube had reached her stomach.

The nurse closest to her nodded to the other, who came up behind her shoulder.

'All right, now, Sharon, this is going to get rid of all that muck you've been filling yourself up with.'

One of them held the tube high above her head, while the second poured water into it. Sharon was aware of the water reaching the end of the tube and then she was jerking her head forward hard. She was going to be sick!

The nurse lowered the tube over a plastic bucket and a thin, off-white liquid squirted into the bottom. Sharon's eyes were half-closed, watering, beginning to smart.

She sensed the tube being lifted up again; more water being poured in. Almost at once the tube was brought down to the bucket. I can't, thought Sharon. I can't!

A third time.

And each time it was worse; each time it seemed as if she could feed nothing more of herself into that tube; each time she did. She struggled to free her hands, wanting to yank the thing from her throat and hurl it across the room. Her hands were gripped tight.

'That's the way, love. Keep it coming.'

Sharon's right shoulder was numb. She felt as though the lining of her stomach was being ripped away, a piece at a time. Through the blur she could see, floating in the bucket, tiny pieces of aspirin.

Dribble was running from the sides of her mouth down on

to the plastic sheeting, on to the neck of the thing she was wearing. She wanted to wipe it away. Wanted one of the nurses to wipe it for her.

But no : again the tube. And again.

It went on for a long time.

It went on until not a particle of the tablets remained in her stomach.

'Okay, now, Sharon. Let's have this thing away from you.'

Sharon opened her mouth as wide as she could, yielding it up to them. When the tube had been removed, her first feeling was of a huge space inside herself that had been hollowed out and then left empty.

She realized that the man had let go of her hands ; reached slowly round and wiped at her mouth.

'She'll be all right, Mrs Holmes. You don't have to worry.'

Sharon saw her mother's face. What was her mother doing there?

'Sharon, love, I'm sorry. I'm sorry!'

She knew that her mother was crying.

'We'll have to move her now, Mrs Holmes. You'll be able to see your daughter upstairs.'

They started to push the bed out of the room. Sharon touched one of the female nurses on the arm. 'I need to go to the toilet.'

Her voice was so weak she was certain the nurse wouldn't have heard it.

The face leaned over her as they went along : 'You'll have to wait until we're upstairs in the ward. You can go then. Just hang on to it, there's a good girl.'

Sharon nodded briefly, closed her eyes. She wanted to go badly ; she really did. Her tummy felt as though it was bursting.

The lift doors slid shut and they rose up. It was very quick. The next thing she was being pushed down the middle of a ward, beds on either side, people looking at her. One bed with curtains drawn round it.

'Careful, now.'

Two of them eased her from the one bed to the other.

'Nurse. Nurse!'

'What is it?'

'Toilet.'

The nurse who had held the tube helped her off the bed and across the ward. She held the cubicle door open for her.

'In you go, then. I'll have to leave this open.'

Sharon's eyes protested.

'You'll be very weak after that lot. Don't want you collapsing in there and no one knowing. I'll be back in a sec.'

Sharon sat on the toilet, holding the seat with one hand, the front of her stomach with the other, looking out through the open door into the ward.

After a moment one of the other nurses came into the toilet with a bottle.

'Have you got enough left to let us have some in here?'

Tucked up in bed, two pillows behind her head, Sharon asked what the urine sample had been for.

'Oh, nothing to worry yourself about.'

'But what?'

'Just a pregnancy test. Routine.'

The nurse smiled, smoothed down the sheet, and walked away down the ward.

At three o'clock, Sharon said yes to tea but no to a piece of cake or a slice of bread and jam. The tea was weak and only lukewarm. She sipped at it and ended up leaving two thirds. No, thanks, she didn't want a second cup.

Sharon put the magazine the woman in the next bed had given her on to the top of the locker and lay back. Down the ward, on the opposite side, someone was coughing. She'd been coughing off and on ever since the morning.

Sharon lay her head to one side, eyes shut. She was glad, now, to be left on her own.

Her mother had been with her, earlier in the day. She'd sat close to the bed, her eyes showing how much she'd been crying. Sharon herself, once in the ward, had not cried at all. There was nothing there : vacant.

On and on, her mum had gone, round and round. How it was her fault, how she should have realized what was going on, that things would be better. A sniff, a dab with a tissue, and then – why had she done it? Why hadn't she talked to someone, talked to her? She was her mother, wasn't she?

Yes, Sharon had thought, yes.

The sister had come and suggested to Mrs Holmes that it might be better if she went home and came back in the evening. After seven. Sharon could do with a rest. Mrs Holmes might appreciate a rest herself. It had been a trying day.

Soon after that one of the doctors had come and taken a blood sample. The prick in her skin had made her eyes water.

'Be brave. We want to see whether any of that stuff got into your blood stream. If it has we'll have to keep an eye on it. That will mean a few more of these, I'm afraid.'

It had. They took blood samples every hour after that.

The next thing was a glucose drip. Fitting the needle into her arm, the blood spurted up into the air and splashed down over the bedcover and the sheet. Some of it went on the doctor's arm, on to the dark hair beneath his wrist.

Sharon had jumped, looked frightened.

'Don't you go worrying about that. A little drop of blood won't hurt either of us.'

A nurse strapped up her arm.

'Be careful not to pull on that now. You don't want to be having that thing out of there.'

The spots of her blood were still on the bedclothes, drying darkly. They were still to be there when she finally came out of the hospital, three days later.

Her father came by himself that first evening.

'Your mum was too upset,' he said apologetically, 'she sends her love. She'll be in to see you tomorrow.'

He held out a bag of grapes for Sharon to see, then put them in the bowl on her locker.

'I didn't know till I got home from work. They'd only phoned your mum from the school. Her name was on the form or something like that. Person to contact in case of accident.' He glanced across at her quickly. 'She told me as soon as I got in. I didn't know what to say. What to think. It really poleaxed me, I don't mind admitting it.'

Sharon tried to move more to one side and winced.

'I was going to come straight round, but your mum said it was best to wait for the proper visiting, so I . . . so I had some tea first.'

He chuckled self-consciously.

'Have you had your tea yet?'

Sharon shook her head.

'Late, isn't it?'

'I didn't want any.'

'No, well, I don't suppose you did, if I think about it. To-morrow, maybe.'

Mr Holmes nodded, looked round the ward.

'Did you . . .' He pulled his chair closer to the bed, lowered his voice. 'Did you, well, do it over what happened when you ran off to London? Was that what it was? Was it?'

'I don't know, dad. It was a lot of things. I don't know now. I can't think.'

'All right, love. When you're feeling stronger will do.'

Mr Holmes sighed, undid the buttons of his coat, then did them up again. He kept glancing round as if not wanting anyone he knew to see him there.

'She's taken it very hard, you know, your mum. Really up-set, she is. Blaming herself. All the time. Blaming herself. I kept telling her, it's not your fault, Maureen, it's not your fault, but she wouldn't listen. You'll have to tell her yourself tomorrow when she comes in. If she hears it from you it'll be different. No sense in making herself ill over it, is there?'

Sharon turned her head on the pillow, looked away.

'Sharon. Sharon?'

He stood up and bent across the bed, looking down at her face. 'Sharon?'

Sharon continued to stare down the ward, seeing nothing.

9

The card had been left downstairs at reception and brought up to the ward by one of the porters. He had grinned when he gave her the envelope and showed a broken front tooth. Said something about it coming from her boy-friend, but he was foreign and Sharon hadn't been able to understand him clearly.

The picture on the front showed a pretty young girl with blonde hair tied up in a pony tail. She was wearing a blue and white check dress that came almost to the ground and she was doing some kind of dance. There were flowers scattered about – daisies and things.

Above her head, in large imitation handwriting, were the words : *Get Well Soon.*

All of the form had signed it inside. Even Debbie. Miss Keble's signature was there, too. Margaret Keble. Small, neat letters, with a curl at the bottom of the M as well as the K.

Sharon thought about her buying the card on the way home the previous night, perhaps at Smith's in the town centre, or on the way in that morning. Passing it round during registration and saying how important it was to write clearly and not to smudge it. She had probably made an announcement beforehand, although everyone would have known, of course.

Sharon could picture the expression on the teacher's face, hear the voice she used whenever she was really being serious. Like the time one of the girls, Denise, had got pregnant.

'Right, now I want you all to listen carefully and without any fuss.'

Denise sitting at the back of the room all the time, next to her best friend, Lynne. Everyone pretending not to stare at her, peeking under their arms, round their shoulders.

There'd been this stunned silence, then Carol had called out : 'Oh, that's lovely!'

All the girls had started talking then, some to each other in little huddles, some to Denise, saying, 'Congratulations! Congratulations!'

Miss Keble had let it go on for a few minutes, then demanded silence once more. She went on to talk about how long Denise was going to stay on at school and how everyone should be careful with her and stuff like that.

Sharon hadn't been able to believe it at first. Hadn't believed it for a long time. She just couldn't imagine Denise, well, doing it. Going with a boy like that.

The others, the ones who were out every night up Bowes Lyon House or the Mecca, it wouldn't have surprised her if it had been one of them who'd fallen for it. Made themselves sound like right little sluts, sometimes. Bragging about it. Not caring who heard them.

But Denise...

Sharon caught herself looking at her after that, trying to work it out. And she wasn't the only one. The boys, too, they kept sneaking glances at her, making jokes to themselves behind their hands, laughing.

Debbie and Heather and them were all round her, one minute being kind and offering to knit things, the next really digging for as much dirt as they could get.

Denise's friend, Lynne, she hardly said a thing. She went around with her just as much as before, but she never seemed pleased about it. About Denise being pregnant. As though she was jealous.

Heather made a joke about that. She said that Denise and Lynne were so close that whoever the bloke was, he would have been forced to have Denise with Lynne looking on.

'That wouldn't 'ave mattered,' Debbie had laughed, 'silly cow wouldn't 'ave known what 'e was doin' anyway.'

That was the other thing, thought Sharon. Nobody knew who the bloke was. Except for Denise herself, of course. And she wasn't telling.

No matter what other people said, her parents, friends, the teachers, the welfare, what arguments they used, Denise refused to say who it had been. Who the father was.

She would sit there without an expression on her round, splodgy face, lips pursed, silent.

It didn't seem right to Sharon. After all, it was at least his responsibility as much as hers. More so. And what about the baby? It wasn't being given any choice as to whether it had a dad or not. Later would be too late. It wasn't right to be without a dad.

There was something about Denise's stubbornness, though, that Sharon admired. Just sitting there, saying nothing, yet telling the whole world to piss off.

She would have liked to have said that to the nurse who'd taken a urine sample to give her a pregnancy test. She wished she'd dared.

Bloody cheek!

The same nurse had come waltzing through the ward earlier that day. 'It's all right,' she'd said when she came by Sharon's bed, 'you don't have to worry. You're not pregnant.'

When the sister had been along later to see how she was feeling and to check her chart, Sharon had asked her about the test.

'Will you tell me mum about that?'

The sister had looked at her, not showing that she understood.

'I mean, if she hears you did that, she'll think, well, you know, she'll think there was a reason for it. She will.'

'Don't fret. It's only routine. Unfortunately pregnancy is such a common cause of young girls taking an overdose, we do it automatically.'

She had clipped the chart back on the end of the bed.

'There's no need to say anything to your mother. It was negative, after all.'

Sharon sat with her back propped up by three pillows and her arm resting on another. It was kept straight by a plastic splint while the glucose drip was still needed. The nurse had said she should be able to do without it by the next day. Already they were taking blood samples less frequently. The amount of aspirin in her blood stream was small and reducing.

'Lucky girl, aren't you?' they kept saying. 'Lucky young girl.'

'How old are you? Only fifteen? Fancy you doing a thing like that at your age! What d'you want to go and do a thing like that for, young girl like you? Upsetting everyone.'

That was it, Sharon thought, she'd been upsetting everyone. She'd been thoughtless. She'd made her mother ill, wasn't that what her father had said? Nothing about what anybody had made her.

Sharon sat there feeling angry and hurt and stupidly, stupidly guilty.

She took the card and put it away in the drawer of her locker.

Sharon had been getting increasingly bored. The woman in the next bed had lent her some more magazines, chatted for a bit; mostly she'd gone on about her diabetes. A lot of them in the ward seemed to have that.

There were one or two patients with eczema; one with this vivid purple rash that started immediately beneath the line of her hair and went down her face and body, disappearing inside the top of her nightie.

Nothing seemed to have happened; nothing had changed. Not really. The pills had gone; she didn't even feel ill any more, only a sore stomach whenever she thought about it.

Was that all there was, then?

Sitting in the hospital bed like that, fed up.

So Sharon was quite relieved when the man came to talk to her. He was tall, stocky; around forty, she imagined. He wore a check suit in that kind of cloth that has little wisps of hair all over it. Dark green and brown. Glasses with thick frames that he took off as soon as he sat down and pushed into the end of a case in his top pocket.

He crossed his legs and tapped a finger on some papers held on a clip board. 'Well, Sharon Irene.' He smiled. 'Sharon, you like to be called, I expect. Is that right?'

Sharon nodded and mumbled, 'Yes.' She hated it when anyone used her middle name. Why had he done that?

'How are you feeling today?'

'All right.'

'Tummy better? Stopped aching?'

'Umm.'

'That's good.'

He drummed his fingers on the board and glanced down the ward. 'I expect you're starting to get bored. Be glad to go home, leave us behind.'

'Yes.'

He smiled again : it was a nice smile, open; he had even, white teeth. Sharon thought for a moment that he looked like one of those dentists in the television adverts, encouraging you to buy toothpaste.

'Now, Sharon, I shall want to ask you one or two questions.'

She shifted her head to one side. 'What about?'

'About what happened to you the other day. About why you're here. It won't take long. I . . .'

'Are you a doctor?'

He uncrossed his legs. 'No, not exactly. Not in the way I expect you mean. I don't mend broken bones or . . .' and he smiled once more '. . . broken tummies.'

'Are you a psychiatrist, then?'

'If you like.'

If she liked – what did that mean?

'You've had time to think about it now. Why you took all those tablets. Why do you think it was, Sharon?'

She said nothing for a long time. The psychiatrist waited patiently, not fidgeting. Around them the business of the ward went on.

'I was ... I don't know ... everything was ...'

'Getting on top of you?' he offered.

'Yes.'

'At school or outside?'

'Everything.'

'It wasn't just work then? Exams coming up – that sort of thing?'

She shook her head.

'I talked to your parents. They're very concerned about you, you know.'

Sharon looked past the psychiatrist's shoulder; one of the Indian nurses was pushing a trolley laden with instruments and different shaped metal trays and dishes.

He leaned forward, placing the clip board on the end of the bed. 'You do know that, don't you, Sharon?'

'What?'

'That your parents are concerned about you.'

She said, 'Yes' in a tone of voice that suggested she didn't mean it.

'You don't get on with them very well?'

Sharon shrugged : 'It's all right.'

'But you did run away?'

'Yes. I was going to me nan's.'

'You like your nan?'

'Yes, she's really nice, my nan.'

'But you didn't get to see her?'

Sharon looked at the shape of her knees under the bed clothes. 'I came back.'

'Why did you do that, Sharon?'

'I ... I ...' She remembered the events at the station.

'I . . .' She wasn't going to say that she had been frightened, terrified.

She waited for the man to ask her again, but all he said was, 'Well, never mind that for now. Perhaps we can talk about it later.'

Sharon looked back up at him; he used finger and thumb to pull his glasses from their case and shake them open. He picked up his notes and looked at them. Later, Sharon thought, later. Why was she having to see him again? There wasn't anything wrong with her – that sort of wrong.

'Sharon, when you took those tablets, what did you think would happen?'

She pushed at her brown hair, moving a strand away from the corner of her mouth.

'Did you think about it?'

Why did he keep on, asking questions? She didn't want to think about it. Not any more. It had happened : wasn't that enough?

'All right, then, Sharon. That will do for today.' He was standing by the end of the bed, board tucked under his right arm. 'The sister will make an appointment for you to come and see me.' He smiled : 'I shall look forward to it.'

He went off down the ward, stopping to speak with the sister on the way.

Teresa came that evening. Well, late afternoon really. She'd taken an evening off from her cleaning job. Specially. Sharon was really pleased. Excited.

And she didn't come alone.

She walked slowly up the ward, looking from one bed to the next, almost pulling Lol along behind her. They were both carrying crash helmets.

'Hello, Sharon. How you feelin'?' Teresa pointed : 'This is Lol.'

Sharon blushed; looked away. They sat down, next to one another at the same side of the bed. Opposite the drip.

'Forcible feedin', is it?' asked Lol, nodding at it. 'There's a law against that, you know.'

'It's a drip,' said Sharon, quietly.

'Oo you callin' a drip?' Loudly.

Teresa took a white paper-bag out of her helmet. 'We brought you some chocolate.' She handed Sharon the bag. There was a bar of milk chocolate inside. Sharon broke off two pieces and offered them to Teresa and Lol.

'We did 'ave two bars for you,' said Lol, straight-faced, 'but Teresa ate the other one on the way up in the lift.'

'You rotten liar!' She thumped Lol on the shoulder and he groaned as if in agony and half-fell to the floor.

A nurse stopped at the end of the bed and tutted.

'Ow, nurse! Me arm! She's broken me arm.'

Sharon had one hand to her mouth, trying to stop herself from laughing too much. Teresa pretended to look annoyed, enjoying it really. A laugh, Lol was. That was one of the reasons she liked him.

'I'm glad you could come,' said Sharon, still giggling.

'Gettin' fed up, are you?'

'Yea.'

Sharon told them all about her visit from the psychiatrist, about the nurses, the other patients.

''Ere,' said Lol looking round, 'what's up with that old girl over there?'

'Which one?'

'Her as looks like one of the brides of Dracula.'

'Lol, don't, she'll hear you.'

'Leave it out! She's past 'earin' anything.'

He stuck his front teeth out over his lower lip and pretended to sink his fangs into Teresa's neck. 'Blood! I must have blood!'

Sharon laughed until her stomach hurt.

'For heaven's sake, Lol! This is an 'ospital.'

'No! I've come to the wrong place, then. There's nothin' wrong with me.'

'That's what you think. You should take a look at yourself from where I'm sitting.' Teresa turned to Sharon. 'What do you think, Sharon?'

'He looks all right to me,' she said, and then blushed twice as deeply as before.

'You want to take it easy with that chocolate,' said Lol, as Sharon was breaking off another piece. 'You know what 'appens to you when you get carried away with what you're eatin'.' He pointed to the bed, the drip. 'You get indigestion somethin' rotten!'

Sharon saw her parents arriving at the far end of the ward. 'It's me mum and dad. You can stay if you like. They won't say anything.'

'No, it's all right. We'll be goin'. I'll see you at school next week, I expect.'

'Yea, see you,' said Lol.

'See you. Bye, Teresa.'

'Bye.'

School next week. Sharon wondered what it would be like. Thinking about it, she came to dread it.

'Hello, love.' Kiss.

'Hello, Mum.' Pause.

'Hello, Dad.'

'Hello, Sharon. How're you feeling?' He pecked at her, touching his lips briefly to the side of her face, in front of her ear.

For three quarters of an hour they talked about nothing very special, with increasingly long gaps in between. Her dad had brought her some apples and oranges to go with the grapes.

'You didn't ask how your mum is. She's feeling better to-day, aren't you, Maureen?'

Her mother seemed to be holding herself in, sitting un-usually straight-backed, paler than normal. Sharon thought she wanted one of her cigarettes; that was what she looked like.

'Nurse says you'll be able to come home the day after to-morrow.'

'Staff nurse,' put in Mrs Holmes.

"Er, yes. Staff nurse. She told us on the way in. When you were talking to your friends. From your school are they?'

'Teresa is. Lol's her boyfriend.'

'What sort of a name is that?' asked Mrs Holmes.

'It's Laurence, really. He's nice.'

Mrs Holmes almost shuddered : 'All that greasy hair.'

'Pal of yours is she?' her father asked. 'This Teresa.'

'Yes,' said Sharon. 'Yes, she is.'

'Nice of her to come.'

'Never heard you mention her before,' her mother said.

Her dad went round and picked up the bowl to offer them grapes. He gave some to the woman in the adjoining bed as well.

'When you get home,' he said, lowering his voice, 'we'll talk. The three of us. Together. Get things sorted out. Make sure it doesn't happen again. Won't we, Maureen?'

'Yes. Yes. So you say. We shall have to do something.'

He flashed her a look and for a moment Sharon thought he was going to really have a go at her. But he let it pass.

'We talked to the psychiatrist the other day. He said he was going to see you.' Mrs Holmes was standing up, doing up the buttons of her green coat, large white buttons. 'Have you seen him yet?'

'Yes.'

'Get on all right, did you?' asked her dad.

Sharon shrugged her shoulders. 'S'pose.'

'He's only trying to help, love. Try and tell him what he wants to know.'

For some reason Sharon could see her mother tightening her lips. Her dad bent down and kissed her quickly on the top of her head; her mother pecked at her cheek, then paused.

'Whatever that psychiatrist says, Sharon, you've got to

remember one thing. What you did caused a lot of trouble and upset. It was just childish, Sharon. Very childish, indeed.'

10

'Mr Loman won't be a minute.' The secretary stepped back into her office, closing the door behind her. Miss Keble stood for a moment in the centre of the room; there was a large green pot plant on one edge of the headmaster's desk, a set of stacked trays for correspondence at the other. She was just pulling a chair from the corner when the door opened.

'Sorry I'm late. You haven't been waiting long?'

'No, Mr Loman.'

'Good, good.'

The headmaster was in his early fifties; he dressed as he always did – a dark two-piece suit, a shirt that was light in colour but not actually white, a tie in muted stripes.

He took an envelope from one of the dark green trays and extracted a form. 'I have the report from the hospital on Sharon Holmes.' He held it high for a moment, as if proving its existence. 'The member of the psychiatric staff who dealt with her is particularly interesting.'

Miss Keble shifted forward on her chair.

'According to him, she had no clear-cut reasons for doing what she did. He certainly didn't think she intended to take her life.' He looked at Miss Keble directly. 'But then, that sort of girl, they rarely do.'

Miss Keble stared at the carpet and said nothing.

'He wasn't very impressed with her at all, actually. He made it clear to her that he thought her actions had been thoughtless and that she'd achieved nothing other than making a lot of worry for her parents and taking up a bed and the time of the hospital staff who have more important things to do.'

'Isn't that possibly rather strong?'

'Not at all. Exactly the right approach, in my opinion. What girls like Sharon need is some straight talking to. Knock them out of their self-indulgence.'

Miss Keble crossed then uncrossed her legs; she started to say something then stopped.

Mr Loman put down the papers on his desk. 'How does she seem now she's back?'

'It's difficult to say. Especially with Sharon. She's not very good at showing what she's feeling at the best of times. She's always kept herself pretty much to herself. I was really surprised when this happened.'

'You had no idea?'

'No, not really.'

From the way the head looked at her, Miss Keble got the impression she had just taken a further step down in his estimation.

'The parents – have you made any contact. Since, er . . .'

'I went round to the house and talked to them. To Sharon as well. It's pretty clear they'd been putting a lot of pressure on her to do well in the exams.'

'Without a great deal of success, I gather?'

'Her parents were thinking in terms of her passing six or eight O-levels. I'm afraid they were making an unrealistic forecast for her to live up to.'

'Hmm. They don't come to parents' evenings, I suppose?'

'They came this last time. But, no, not as a rule.'

Mr Loman sighed : 'It's always the same story – the ones you want to see most . . .'

He left the sentence unfinished; glanced at the hospital report, folded it carefully. 'Why do you think she took this overdose?'

Miss Keble adjusted the hem of her skirt. 'I'm not sure. She was worried about her exams, that was one thing. Then her parents were trying to be stricter with her. Checking up on her. Making sure she stayed in and worked.'

'No boy-friend? Usually, in these sort of cases they loom a lot larger than work.'

'Her mother said something about a boy, but it didn't sound too serious.'

'And Sharon?'

'She denied it.'

'Yes, well ...' Mr Loman gestured with his hand, then leant back in his chair, elbows resting on the arms. 'There's one more appointment with the psychiatrist. After that she'll probably be referred to one of the county educational psychologists. Oh, and I've talked to Mr Dawson about her French. That was one of the bones of contention, I believe?'

'Yes.'

'Well, Mr Dawson has kindly agreed to let her drop from the set. Doubtless, there's work she can be catching up on. Perhaps you could arrange that, Miss Keble?'

'Of course, I ...'

'And if you could make an appointment for her parents to visit the local employment officer, take the girl with them. Possible careers, further education courses, that sort of thing.'

'Yes, Mr Loman.'

'Very well,' the headmaster stood up. 'Let's hope that now she's got it out of her system, she'll settle down.'

Miss Keble was still sitting, looking up at him.

'There wasn't anything else?'

'No, Mr Loman.' She stood up, pushing the chair back. 'No.'

'Good. Good.'

He went across and opened the door that led out into the corridor. Two boys nearly knocked into her, running. She turned her head and called after them, hearing the running begin again as soon as she was out of sight.

Why hadn't she said what she was thinking? That the only reason Sharon had ended up in so many O-level groups was that she had been put into them lower down the school. After the third year the number of pupils moved was minimal. Like saying they don't change after that and neither will we.

Which meant that at least some part of the responsibility was theirs.

Miss Keble stopped at the foot of the staff room stairs. If they were to re-examine their procedures of assessment and ... she could imagine Mr Loman heming and hurrying on to the next item of business. Someone like Mr Dawson being sarcastic about changing the whole school on account of one not very intelligent and highly hysterical girl.

She looked at her watch; there wasn't really time to get a cup of tea before the bell. Miss Keble walked off towards her classroom.

The Norton swung under the main road and roared through the tunnel. Lol twisted the throttle open with his right hand, bringing up his head as they came out into the air. He skidded the bike into a half circle and they came to a halt on the grass. The wheels had gouged arcs into the ground.

Sharon was still clinging to him, her body shaking.

Lol unclipped the strap of his helmet and pulled it off, hanging it on one end of the handlebars. He waved to Teresa, back on the far side of the road.

Lol turned round. 'Enjoy that, did you?'

'Yes,' she said, nodding her head inside Teresa's helmet. 'Yes.'

Lol smiled. 'Let's be gettin' back, then. I fancy a drink.'

He jammed his helmet into place and they raced back through the underpass. When they turned the corner to where Teresa was waiting, Sharon's eyes were shut tight.

Later Lol bought three cans of lager and they sat on the grass by the water tower, not minding that it was damp.

'Good fun, isn't it?' said Teresa.

'Smashing.'

'Frightened, was you?'

Sharon didn't say anything.

'Not much,' said Lol. 'I could feel 'er 'eart thumpin' more than the engine.' He laughed : 'Sharon Holmes. The only girl with a 500 c.c. circulation!'

Lol lit up a cigarette.

'I ought to be gettin' back,' Sharon said.

She got up and walked over to the litter bin to throw away the cans. When she turned to come back, Lol had his arms round Teresa and they were kissing.

'Come out with us Sunday,' said Teresa.

'No. No, I can't.'

'Why not?'

'It's not fair on you. On Lol.'

'Course it is. I don't care. I might be able to borrow me old man's car. We'll go out for the day.'

Sharon thought she must be grinning like an idiot.

'All right. Ta! See you tomorrow, Teresa.'

'Yea. See you.'

Sharon ran across the field, past the football posts. It wasn't until she got home and was turning the key in the front door that she remembered tomorrow was the day she had to go to see the psychiatrist.

Sharon got off the bus one stop before she should, before she needed. It was a funny sort of afternoon, neither one thing nor the other. The sky was a pasty white, stretched through here and there with lines of grey. It was cold enough for Sharon to have her coat on, one hand holding the flaps together near the top.

She wandered along the path, going as slowly as she could without actually stopping. She guessed that she must be ten minutes late already. Good. The later she was the better. If she dawdled long enough the session would be more than half over. And this was the last one. Unless he'd changed his mind.

She wondered if the psychiatrist saw any more point to their meetings than she did. He was nice enough, chatting about school and things, smiling his toothpaste smile; never losing his temper when she sat there gazing at his desk, not answering.

Nice enough, but – whatever he said, it came back to questions. Questions she didn't want to answer. Things she wasn't prepared to tell him. Private things. Personal.

Sharon stopped and looked at the school buildings on her left. The Catholic Girls' School. Someone in a blue cardigan walking along a corridor, scratching the back of her head. In one of the classrooms, rows of girls, cut off at the waist where the glass became wall. The teacher was writing something on a board, stopping every minute or so to look round and say something to the class.

Sharon yawned; tried to read what was written on the board but she was too far away.

She wondered if that school were any different from her own, if she would have got on better if she'd gone somewhere else. It didn't matter. Not now. In less than a year she would have left.

She waited to cross the road. A line of cars was going past, heading for the motorway roundabout. A small boy waved at Sharon from the back window of one, waving and smiling. By the time Sharon waved back, he was lost from sight behind the following car.

She ran to the other side of the road, still holding on to her coat.

She could have cut across the grass to the hospital, but she didn't; took the longer way round by the path.

He wasn't daft, the psychiatrist. He knew there was something else apart from her school work that had been worrying her, upsetting her. More even than the rows at home, her parents keeping her in. That was what he kept digging away at, trying to prise it out of her. But Sharon clung to it tightly, not even sure herself what it was. How she would put it into words, even if she wanted to. ·

It wasn't Mick. Since she'd been in the hospital, she'd

hardly thought about him. It wasn't that stupid Debbie. It was – oh, who knew what it was?

Sharon kicked at a stone in front of her and it went skipping across the service road that led into the hospital. Down past the road they were pulling down the old pub and rebuilding it. She'd gone there once with her parents. On a Sunday. Last summer, she supposed it had been.

There was a garden at one side and at the back. On a slope. People sitting on the grass, on benches and chairs, all over. Because it was outside, children were allowed. There were lots of them, running around and shouting until they knocked over someone's drink and then their dad would come after them, give them a good telling off and a slap. Kids and dogs.

She'd sat between her mum and dad. Her mum on a chair with wooden slats, her and her dad on the grass.

'Mind you don't stain that dress!'

A bottle of Pepsi-Cola and a bag of crisps.

One of the workmen saw Sharon standing by the side of the road and whistled, raising his arm and bending it upwards at the elbow. She went on towards the hospital.

Less than a quarter of an hour after walking into the psychiatrist's office, she was walking out again.

'You're late,' he'd said, holding the end of one side of his glasses. But he hadn't seemed surprised.

At the end, he'd got up and opened the door for her. Smiling at her as she hesitated, unsure of what to say.

''Bye, Sharon. Look after yourself. It's been nice talking with you.'

She blushed, mumbled something and hurried out. The door closed behind her.

On her way to the exit, she saw a girl sitting at the end of a long bench seat, wearing a white raincoat. It was Alison Westford, the prefect from school. Her arms were by her sides, folded neatly, hands forward – as though someone had put her there, carefully.

Sharon stood there, wondering whether she should say

something or walk past and pretend she hadn't noticed.

As she was hesitating, Alison turned her head towards her. 'Hello.'

That was it, then. She walked over there and stood beside her.

Alison looked up at her. 'How are you feeling?'

'I'm okay, thanks.'

'I heard about what happened.'

Sharon hung her head a little, nodded.

'I'm sorry.'

Sharon pursed her lips; she didn't know what to say.

'That day in the cloakroom – was it anything to do with that?'

'No. Yes. Oh, sort of. It . . . it doesn't matter.'

She didn't feel she could just walk away.

'Are you visiting someone?' she asked, finally.

'No. No, I'm here as a patient.'

'Oh, I'm sorry. I didn't know.' Sharon felt even more awkward, flustered. 'What's the matter?'

Alison moved one of her hands; looked up at Sharon, for an instant uncertain. 'I'm seeing a psychiatrist.'

'You are!' Sharon realized that she said it too loudly. She glanced quickly over her shoulder, going red again.

Alison pretended not to notice. 'Yes. I've just come out. I usually sit here for a while afterwards. Coming round, I suppose. I find it tiring. It drains me.'

'I . . . that's where I've been. Because of what happened, they thought . . . It was my last time.'

'You're lucky. I've been going for ages. It appears to be never-ending.'

Sharon fidgeted from one foot to the other. What was a girl like Alison Westwood doing going to a psychiatrist? She was really clever, in the upper sixth and everything.

A man came and sat down at the other end of the seat.

'We can get a cup of tea,' Alison said, standing up. 'Before the next bus. If you like.'

Sharon was uncertain; she would rather have gone on back. But because Alison had started walking down the corridor and was obviously expecting her to follow, she did so.

The tea was strong. Sharon put in an extra spoonful of sugar, stirred it hard.

'What's yours like?' Alison asked.

'He's not bad. Nice really. Only . . .'

'Only what?'

Sharon made a face. 'He's always prying into things that aren't his business. I'm not going to talk about things like that to someone I don't know. It isn't right. He isn't anything to me.'

Alison opened her mouth to say something, but stopped.

'What about your bloke?' Sharon asked.

Alison put down her cup. 'It's a woman. She's fine. Very patient, compassionate. Doesn't get upset if things seem to be taking a backward step. I think perhaps I'm addicted to her. Just like the valium. It's like being on a treadmill. Once you're on, it's impossible to get off. Ibsen should have written a play about it.'

'Eh?'

'Oh, sorry. Thinking aloud. Forget it.' She drank some more of her tea. 'You're pleased you're not going again, then, are you?'

'There didn't seem to be any point. I just wanted to get it over.'

She was surprised to see the sixth former smiling at her. 'Perhaps you're right.'

Mr Holmes sat in his usual chair, feet resting on a cushion which he'd put on the little table. He was wearing the same old trousers, the same cardigan he always wore round the house.

Sharon sat on the far side of the fire, leaning back in the other armchair. Her mother was out. The standard lamp in the corner was on; one bar of the fire : they were watching television.

On the screen a boy of about fifteen was shouting at a man holding a gun. The boy was wearing a torn denim jacket with patches sewn to it. He had a Scottish accent.

Sharon wasn't really interested in the programme, bit stupid really. But her dad usually watched it and she was quite happy, just sitting there. She'd hardly been out since it had happened. Not in the evenings. Her parents would have let her; they'd said so. Well, her dad had. As long as they knew where she was going. She hadn't wanted to. Nowhere to go. Bowes was always the same and there wasn't anywhere else much. The bowling-alley or the Mecca. They were best if you went with a lot of others.

She had thought about going round to Teresa's one evening. Teresa had said. But Sharon was afraid she'd be in the way, with her and Lol and that.

There was a disco up the school on the Saturday, though. She thought she might go to that.

The man on the television was sitting at the foot of a tree. A small girl was holding a bow and arrow, pointing it at him. Sharon couldn't see if the man was tied to the tree or not.

'Sharon?'

'Yea.'

He frowned at her and smiled. 'Sorry! Yes.'

'Things easier at school now, are they? You don't feel so worried?'

'No, Dad. It's all right. Well, better. Dawson stopped getting on at me all the time. And some of the others.'

'Does that include your mum and me?'

Sharon didn't say anything, pretended to be watching the television. The Scottish boy was leading a band of kids across a field, shouting and banging and waving sticks. She couldn't stop herself smiling a little.

'This isn't very good this week. You watching it?'

'No, thought you were.'

'I was.' He got up and switched off the set. The picture twirled to nothingness.

Her dad stood in front of the settee. 'Look, you do still want to leave school in the summer?' He sounded hesitant, apologetic almost. 'That teacher, she said you could go back and take some more ...' He stopped. She could see the concern on his face and suddenly, for no reason she could understand, Sharon wanted to laugh. '... more O-levels.'

'Don't look so worried,' she said, 'I'm not goin' to rush out and swallow another bottle of aspirins just 'cause you mention it. All right?'

Mr Holmes sat down in his chair. 'Yes, I'm sorry.'

'But I don't want to stay on. I really don't.'

'Whatever you say. It's your decision.' He picked a small mat off the table, then put it down again. 'Only ...'

'Only what?'

'When we went to see that chap at the employment office. Those courses he was talking about. At Stevenage College, or over at Ware. You sounded interested in those at the time.'

'I was.'

'Have you looked at the booklets he gave you?'

'Yes,' slightly exasperated.

Her dad put one hand to the side of his head. It was just like she did herself, Sharon thought, except that she had hair to push out of the way and he didn't. Funny, she'd never noticed that before.

He stood up and went to the door. Door open, he turned back into the room. 'You're going to have to make up your mind some time, you know.'

She looked up at him. One of the buttons on his cardigan was hanging off by a thread. 'Yes, Dad, I know. I know I will.'

11

Sharon's dad drove her up to the school in the car. She hadn't made up her mind properly until the last moment. Sitting in her room, staring at herself in the mirror; one eye made up, her best dress laid out on the bed behind her. She'd only worn it three times before.

Always the same sounds from downstairs: the television, the kettle being filled, every ten minutes or so voices she couldn't clearly hear.

Sharon had chewed at the knuckle of her finger, elbow resting on the small dressing-table. If she didn't go, what else would she do? She couldn't stay in for ever.

Her dad turned in at the entrance.

'Here'll do, Dad.'

It was too late. He'd gone between the opened double gates and swung the car through a wide circle, stopping by the concrete path that led to the school.

'Thought I might as well deliver you in style.'

Sharon opened the passenger door, one leg out, foot on the ground.

'Sharon?'

'Yea? Yes?'

'You say it finishes at eleven?'

'Yes.'

'I'll be parked on the road, just before the gate. Okay?'

'Yes, Dad.'

She got out of the car and started to shut the door.

'Sharon?'

She sighed, lowered her head and looked into the car.

'Have a good time.'

'I'll try.'

Sharon shut the car door with a bang and walked towards the main school building almost smiling.

Mr Eliot was sitting behind a table inside the entrance to the dining hall, collecting tickets and checking who was coming in. Miss Keble stood behind him, holding a plastic glass of Coke.

'Hello, Sharon,' she said immediately, looking really pleased to see her. 'I hoped you'd come.'

Mr Eliot took her ticket and tore it in half. 'Let's have your hand, then.'

Sharon held out her right hand, palm downwards, and he pressed a rubber stamp down on to the back of it.

Sharon walked away from the table, looking for somewhere to leave her coat. On the back of her hand it said : Property of Hertfordshire County Council.

The disco was in the main hall. The partition between the dining room and the hall had been pulled back and you could see the lights the DJ was using, flashing and changing colour as they bounced off walls and ceiling.

He was playing something by Stevie Wonder.

Sharon bought a Coke and looked around. The room had been decorated with sheets of coloured paper round the lights and spray paintings fixed to the walls. She saw a couple of girls from her class sitting at a table overlooking the hall. She went over and sat with them.

After saying hello, there wasn't much else to talk about : the music was so loud that it didn't matter very much, anyway. Sharon sat there, sipping her drink and tapping her feet, watching what was going on. As yet there weren't many people dancing. Mostly girls. She guessed that those boys who were coming were still in the pub.

Miss Keble came over to the table and sat down for ten minutes or so, chatting to the girls, having to repeat almost everything at least once.

The DJ kept shouting at people to get out on the floor; the lights became more insistent; the two girls with Sharon went down to dance. She pushed her hair away from her face and bit the inside of her lip. What had she come for?

'Sharon! Wotcher!'

Teresa pushed her way through the crowd that had formed in between the tables, Lol alongside her, grinning and holding three glasses of Coke in his hands, trying not to spill any.

'We brought you a drink.' She sat in the chair next to Sharon, shaking her hair loose.

'I haven't finished this yet.'

Lol reached across the table and took her glass, draining what was left in one mouthful. 'You 'ave now!'

He pushed a full glass over to her and grinned more broadly than before. 'Cheer up! 'Snot a bleedin' funeral!'

Sharon smiled and turned to look at what Teresa was wearing. She had a big shawl, black wool, all crocheted. Sharon felt it.

''Sme nan's. She give it me last time I see 'er. Nice i'n'it?'

'It's lovely. I wish I had something like that.'

'Go on. You look smashin'. Doesn't she, Lol?'

'Yea. I can 'ardly control meself.'

Sharon hung her head, blushing and smiling at the same time.

A little while later, they were playing this record by Boz Scaggs and a bloke came over and asked her to dance.

Sharon just sat there, not really looking at him, saying nothing. She felt Teresa's hand on her back, pushing her. 'Go on,' she whispered.

Sharon glanced up at him. Saw a blue suit, open shirt, dark hair. No one she'd ever seen before. No one from school.

'You coming then?'

'Yea, course she is.' That was Teresa.

Sharon nodded and stood up. She followed him down the steps and on to the floor. The record was half way over. He stayed a couple of feet away from her, not moving off the same spot, only dancing with his hips and shoulders really, staring over the top of her head.

Sharon wondered who he was. If he was at school some-where else, or at work. Work, probably. The record finished and she started to move away. He put his hand on her arm.

'Hang about.'

Same sort of tempo. 'I Feel Like Dancing'. That bloke who sounds like a woman. Nice, though. He kept a bit closer this time. There was a small mark on his neck, as though he'd nicked himself shaving. Quite good looking, she supposed. Nothing special, though.

He said something in the middle of the record, but she couldn't hear what it was.

The records changed, one merging into the other. He had both arms round her, pulling her against his chest. The lights had altered, dimmed. Stevie Wonder again. Slow, this time. One hand already on her shoulder, fingers edging across to the back of her neck, touching her skin. The ends of his fingers were rough; hard, round and rough. He pulled her closer still, ducking his head down alongside hers.

The front of him was pressing against her stomach.

Over his shoulder she saw Debbie Bradley and Mick. Mov-ing round and round in a slow circle. Close enough for her to have been able to reach out and touch them. Sharon won-dered how long they'd been there. Whether they'd moved there on purpose. If so, whose idea it had been.

Mick's arms were both round Debbie's neck, hands crossed over at the back, one wrist lying on top of the other. As he turned towards Sharon, he opened his eyes : looked directly at her : through her. Closed his eyes again.

The bloke she was dancing with had pushed his hand down inside the back of her dress, the end of one finger touching her bra strap. Sharon wriggled and he moved his hand up a couple of inches; almost immediately back again.

Mick and Debbie were kissing. Mouths angled to each other; lips obviously open. Mick's cheeks going in and out like he was blowing up a balloon.

The first slow song became another. Sharon tried to move

the pair of them further towards the middle of the floor, not wanting to watch any more.

The hand that wasn't down the back of her dress was resting on her bum. When she moved herself away all she succeeded in doing was pushing herself against him at the front. Immediately his hand held her there, tighter. She could feel his fingers trying to move down inside the elastic of her knickers, from outside her dress. He kissed her neck. Moved his mouth up towards her ear. When his tongue went inside it, she turned her head away fast.

The record stopped. The DJ said something; lights flickered brightly. Some old thing by the Rolling Stones. He was still standing there, one hand back to his own side, the other resting on the top of her shoulder.

'What's yer name?'

'Sharon.'

They were having to shout.

'Wanna go for a walk?'

'Eh?'

'I said, d'you want to go for a wander? Round outside. C'mon.'

Sharon shook her head.

'Whatyer mean?'

She shrugged her shoulders. She felt silly just standing there in the middle of the hall while everyone else was dancing round them.

The fingers squeezed her shoulder. He half turned to move away.

'Come on! You comin' or aren't yer?'

She shook her head again, not really looking at him. 'No.'

'Suit yerself!'

He put up an arm and made a path for himself through the dancers. Sharon waited a moment, then walked round the other way.

'What was all that about?' asked Teresa when she sat down.

'All what?'

'You two, standin' down there an' chattin' away like that. Was 'e proposin', or somethin'?'

'Yea. He wanted me to go outside for a walk.'

Teresa and Lol laughed.

'Didn't you fancy 'im, then?' said Lol.

Sharon shook her head, brushed the hair away from her eyes.

'That's all right,' said Teresa. 'They try it on all the time.'

'Why not?' Lol hung his head to one side. 'Don't try, you don't stand to get anywhere, do you?'

Teresa caught Sharon by the arm. ''Ere, I remember this time I went up Bowes. Before I went out with you.' She stuck her tongue out at Lol. 'This bloke comes up to me and says, "D'you want to come up the multi-storey?"'

Sharon and Lol started laughing.

'No, 'e did, honest.'

'You're pulling my leg.'

'No, I'm not. Smashin' view, 'e says.'

'What did you say?'

'Told 'im to piss off, didn't I?'

'Good for you.'

'Come up the multi-storey! Classic, that is.'

When she'd stopped laughing, Sharon said she'd get some more Cokes. Debbie and Mick were standing by the serving hatch; Heather and Carol and a couple of other boys with them.

Sharon stood at the counter, ignoring them, waiting to be served.

'Aren't you speakin', then?'

Sharon started to blush.

'Too good for us.'

'Say hello to Mick, then. Know 'im, don't you? You know Sharon, Mick. She's the one . . .'

A roar of laughter covered the end of the remark. Sharon

put her money down on the counter top. Why didn't they hurry up and serve her?

'Saw you with that bloke, Sharon. Hands all over the place.'

'Yea, wanted you to go outside, did 'e?'

Giggles. Laughter from the blokes. Mick grinning.

'Three Cokes, please.'

'Why didn't you go with 'im, Sharon?'

'Wasn't good enough for her, was he?'

'Stuck up, is she?' asked one of the boys.

Debbie and Carol fell across one another in a fit of laughter. Sharon took her change and got ready to pick up the drinks. When she turned away from the hatch, Debbie was standing in her way.

'Sharon's a good little girl. Anyone tries to get 'old of 'er, she runs off and tries to do 'erself in.'

Sharon opened her hands, dropping the glasses to the floor. Opened her hands and swung back an arm, slapping Debbie hard across her sneering face.

The crack of the slap; plastic glasses bouncing on the floor; Coke splashing over people's legs. 'Hey, look out!' 'What's goin' on?'

Debbie stared at Sharon, her fingers touching her cheek. Then she pushed her way through the crowd, Heather and Carol following after her.

Sharon stood there, not even aware that she was being looked at. Then she quickly picked up the glasses and put them back on the counter.

'You all right?' asked Teresa, when Sharon sat down. 'You've gone all pale.'

'Yea. I had an accident with the drinks. And I ... and I hit Debbie Bradley round the face.'

'What for?'

'Something she said. About what I did. Before.' Sharon looked at Teresa defiantly. 'I didn't 'alf land her one.'

Teresa smiled: 'Good for you. It's about time someone

sorted out that little bitch. About time you stuck up for your-self an' all.'

'About time we had a Coke,' said Lol, getting up. 'I s'pose I'd better go.'

Sharon sat back. The car was warm. The heater was on full blast.

'Nice time?'

'Okay.'

'Is that all?'

'No, it was good really.'

'Lots there?'

'Um.'

They were passing the police station : Sharon felt the muscles of her stomach tightening. The railway station and the leisure centre. Right at the roundabout. Her dad whist-ling.

'Dad?'

'What?'

'At the dance, there was . . . oh, never mind.'

Leaning across : 'No, go on.'

'It doesn't matter.'

'You've started now, you might as well finish. Besides . . .' Looking at her. '. . . I want to know.'

'There was this girl. She's always been getting on at me, right, and she made this joke about me taking them pills and that.'

'So what did you do?'

'I hit her.'

The car swerved slightly.

'Where?'

'In the dining hall.'

'No, I mean . . .'

'Oh, round the face.'

'Hard?'

'Yes.'

'And what did she do?'

'Went off. I didn't see her again.'

Her dad didn't say anything. She kept trying to catch a glimpse of his face in the lights of the oncoming traffic, but she couldn't tell what he was thinking.

When he was putting the car into the garage at the back of the house, he said, 'What you told me about hitting that girl. I shouldn't tell your mum, if I were you. You know what she's like.' He thought for a moment and then : 'Sounds as if she deserved it, though.'

Yes, Dad, Sharon kept saying to herself as they walked through to the house. Yes. Yes. Yes.

Sharon got up early on Sunday morning. Usually she laid in and her dad would get up at half past nine, make a pot of tea and take it back upstairs to bed. This morning, Sharon took them up a tray : teapot, milk jug, sugar, cups and saucers, spoon.

She'd asked her mum to buy an extra cut loaf so that she could make herself some sandwiches. She was ready a good three quarters of an hour before Teresa arrived.

Sharon saw her walk past the kitchen window. By herself. Lol must be waiting up on the road. Then she saw Teresa's face.

'What is it? What's happened?'

It's Lol, Sharon thought, he's had an accident. She looked into Teresa's face and waited for the answer. Not wanting to hear it. Knowing she must.

'We'll 'ave to go out some other day. I 'ad to come an' tell you. Lol's waitin' for me . . .'

Sharon stared at Teresa's face.

'Tell me,' she said.

Teresa sat down. 'You know that girl you met up the hospital?'

'Alison Westford?'

'Her. I found 'er this morning.'

Something scooped air out of Sharon's lungs.

'What . . .?'

'I went out early. For a walk. Really early. I do sometimes. I went over the lakes. It was nice, then. Sunny. I walked all the way round the big one, where they do the yachting. Turned to go back home. Then something made me walk the other way.'

She glanced quickly at Sharon.

'I went past the bandstand. Over the bridge. Round by the second lake. Past the ducks an' that. Saw this thing floating in the water. White.'

Sharon closed her eyes; squeezed her legs together, tight.

'I went down on to the grass. It was a white raincoat. Floating. All spread out, like. Arms an' all. Takin' off me shoes and wadin' in a bit, I could reach it. Pull it in. When I was doin' that, I saw her. On the bottom. It's not deep, you see. Not there. She was lyin' on her side, sort of curled up. Her name was inside her coat. Stitched inside the collar.

'I stood there lookin' at her. Through the water it looked as if she was moving. Ever so slowly. Like rocking.

'I ran down to the café, but there wasn't anyone there. I 'ad to phone from a box down the road. They told me to wait there. Took me back to show 'em the place. I saw 'em lift her out . . .'

Sharon looked away, out through the window towards the bricks of the house opposite. Couldn't look at Teresa's face.

'I'm sorry. I . . .'

Sharon's dad came round the door, wearing his dressing-gown. He looked quickly from Teresa to Sharon and back again. Put the tray down on the side and went back out again.

'I could make you a cup of tea.'

Teresa stood up. 'No, it's okay. Thanks. Lol'll take me back home.'

123

Sharon stood in the doorway, watching Teresa walk up the path to where Lol was waiting. She was still standing there when they had disappeared from sight.

It was raining, suddenly, raining hard. Sharon stood on the wooden bridge while people scurried past her, heading for the cover of the underpass. She had already been standing there for what she thought must be half an hour. The rain ran down between the collar of her coat and her hair and she did nothing to stop it. Watched it splashing back up from the stream below.

She hadn't had any lunch; hadn't wanted any. Her mum had moaned a bit, but that was all. Then she'd come out for a walk. She hadn't meant to come there, to the lakes.

She didn't think she had.

Sharon started to walk off the bridge, between the lines of trees and bushes, along the path that led to the lakes themselves. Something was making a small seething noise at the centre of her head; small but insistent; never still.

The ground was turning back to mud. Her shoes became clogged in it. She leaned over the edge of the water, gazing down into it, beyond her own reflection, down. The lines of rain sprang back sharply, spat in her face. The whole lake moved, quivered.

Sharon touched the surface of the water; closed her eyes. The sound inside her head increased. She blinked, her vision blurred. She saw on the water something moving, something white. Spread out. Arms spread out.

Sharon reached towards them.

It.

It changed. Her skin quivered, stung by fear. Her reflection twisted, leered. That noise behind her eyes, drowning her.

She screamed and when the scream stopped there was nothing but the sound of the rain. The lake was only water. She turned around and there was nobody in sight. No one.

She stood in all that space : alone.

Sharon went back the way she had gone, feeling the wet-
ness seeping through her clothes and not minding. By the
time she had come through the underpass, the rain had begun
to ease off.

Opposite the garage, she walked round by the allotments.
The earth, where it had been freshly turned, steamed. She
wiped at a bench with her arm and sat down. She was so wet
it hardly mattered. Sharon looked down the hill over the
town. Saw the four tower-blocks, one shorter than the others.
Between two of them the light colour of the big insurance
building caught the sun.

What about it, then? she thought. What about it?

There was a way for her somewhere, she knew that. And
it was up to her to find it.

Being clever wasn't it, she was sure of that. Alison had been
clever. Passed all her exams, stayed in, worked hard, been
accepted at university.

But she wasn't going to end up like some of the others,
either. Sitting behind a check-out all day, or pushing refills
into biros.

There had to be something else.

Didn't there?

After a while, she got up and started to walk home.